For

Bear Fur Hire

Bear Fur Hire
ISBN-13: 978-1519283856
ISBN-10: 1519283857
Copyright © 2015, T. S. Joyce
First electronic publication: November 2015

T. S. Joyce
www.tsjoycewrites.wordpress.com

NOTE FROM THE AUTHOR:
This book is a work of fiction. The names, characters, places, and incidents are products of the writer's imagination or have been used fictitiously and are not to be construed as real. Any resemblance to persons, living or dead, actual events, locale or organizations is entirely coincidental. The author does not have any control over and does not assume any responsibility for third-party websites or their content.

Published in the United States of America
First digital publication: November 2015
First print publication: November 2015

Bear Fur Hire

(Bears Fur Hire, Book 2)

T. S. Joyce

ONE

Lena Rhodes screamed as the plane dipped violently.

"Hang on, I'll get us higher," murmured the soft-spoken man piloting the small, four-seater bush plane. He eased them up toward the dark, churning clouds.

Lena closed her eyes and clutched her camera bag against her stomach. She'd made a huge mistake taking this job, but when the president of *Bucks and Backwoods* magazine offered a lifetime opportunity to photograph some of the most dangerous animals on the planet, how could she refuse? This was the jumping point of her career, right here, in the passenger seat of a death rocket shooting through the air right under a building Alaskan storm. But this wasn't even the most terrifying part of the trip. If she survived the turbulent plane ride, she was going to photograph an animal that had only visited her nightmares. The elusive Alaskan brown bear.

She let off a shuddering moan as her stomach dipped again.

"We're almost there, lady."

"Tobias, is it?" she asked, desperate to take her mind off the horrifying storm swirling above them.

"Mmm," he said, barely audible over the rumbling engine.

"H-how long have you been flying this thing?"

"This thing? One month."

Her eyes flew wide, and she nearly choked on air, but the smile on his face said there was a joke in there somewhere.

"The plane is new, but I've been flying for ten years."

"Oh, my gosh," she said on a relieved breath. "That wasn't funny."

"You don't like flying?"

"I like flying on big commercial jets just fine. They serve alcohol and don't hit turbulence like this."

"Am I your first bush plane flight?"

Panting in panic and squishing herself against the seat, eyes on the ground far below, Lena nodded in short jerks.

"Well, stop your worrying. I've never had a crash, and I fly all the time."

"Do you always fly clients out to Silver Summit Outfitters?"

"No, I don't. I run deliveries all over Alaska, but on occasion, I fly people out here on a favor."

"A favor to whom?"

"My brother."

Lena dragged her attention from the lush greenery below to the man sitting next to her. "Your brother works at Silver Summit?"

The man placed his hand on his chest and said, "Tobias Silver, at your service."

"Whoa, both hands on the wheel!" She drew a long steadying breath. "Your brother owns the lodge?"

"Co-owns it. Have you picked out a guide yet?"

"Uuuuh," she murmured, fumbling for the pamphlet in the satchel at her feet. "I was waiting for a recommendation from my boss. I'm hoping he's left me a message by the time we land."

"What are you here to photograph?"

"Grizzly."

Tobias's dark eyebrows jacked up, and he took his green eyes off the dark sky in front of them to stare at her for way too long for her comfort. "You're going to willingly trek out into brown bear country to *photograph* them?"

"Y-yes."

"Do you know how to shoot?"

"I'm not bringing a rifle, if that's what you mean."

Tobias scratched his neck in what looked like irritation, and when he glanced over at her again, the expression on his face had darkened considerably. "Jenner Silver. Reserve him as your guide."

"Oh, but I checked on him already. He's booked right now, and I was thinking of Chance Dawson or Dalton—"

"No ma'am, you want Jenner. He'll be worth the wait. He can keep you safe."

"Safe how? Because I'm not okay with hurting the animals I photograph."

Tobias huffed a laugh and cast her an *are-you-serious?* look. "I think you'll feel differently when you actually encounter a charging grizzly. And as for my brother's qualifications—let's just say he has a way with the bears."

"What does that mean?"

But Tobias Silver was done talking apparently because he pursed his lips into a thin line and didn't say another word until they reached a long, asphalt landing strip in the middle of nowhere. Only when they were safely on the ground and at a complete stop did her pounding heart rate settle.

Tobias slid out of the plane and jogged around the front as she gathered her belongings. He helped her out and strapped himself down with her bags, equipment, and luggage.

"Thank you for your help," she said.

But Tobias took off into the piney forest without so much as a "you're welcome."

The giant of a man didn't seem to need any directions as he hiked this way and that, following thin, intersecting deer trails through the thick brush until he came to a clearing. But while he strode toward the massive log cabin at the apex of the open field, Lena skidded to a stop in shock.

She'd traveled all over the world and photographed animals in the most beautiful places imaginable, but this right here had her pulse quickening with its beauty.

The lodge was rustic, covered in cedar logs and topped with a red tin roof. A sprawling porch surrounded it, and across the front yard, about a hundred yards away, was a massive deck overlooking a winding, fast-flowing river. On top of the wooden surface were rocking chairs, a wooden swing, and a set of reclined lounge chairs positioned around a wide built-in fire pit. There were snowcapped mountains in the distance, and the clearing was encased in the greenest, thickest pine forest she'd ever seen. Off to the side of the gargantuan lodge was a barn with a trio of horses trotting around a corral.

"You coming or what?" Tobias called in an echoing voice from in front of the lodge.

"Yes, sorry," she said, climbing the sloping mowed yard.

"You all right?" Tobias asked with a worried furrow to his eyebrows.

"I'm fine."

"When women say they're fine, they're not fine. You don't have to do this."

"Do what?" she asked, coming to a stop in front of him and readjusting the single camera bag she carried on her shoulder.

"Go after those grizzlies. You could stay here for a day or two and relax. Maybe take pictures of the black bears that fish the river here. They're safer, you know."

Irritated, she said, "Yes, I know. I've photographed black bears for the past year. Grizzlies are my promotion."

With a judgmental little quirk to his brow, he muttered, "Death by promotion. Your boss sounds like an asshole."

Lena narrowed her eyes at the back of his head as he climbed the porch stairs, but she would not engage. She'd had a long trip here and wasn't up for a row with a stranger who would be out of her life forever in a few minutes.

"You must be Colleen Rhodes," said an older man with a thinning hair line, hunched posture, and a crinkling smile. He held out his hand as she approached the front door. "I'm Lennard Graves, co-owner of Silver Summit Outfitters."

She shook his hand and mirrored his warm smile. "People call me Lena."

"Very good. Nice to meet you Lena." He turned and clapped Tobias on the shoulder, but the giant didn't even sway under the hard hit. "Tobias, it's good to see you again."

"Lennard," Tobias greeted with a nod. "Is my brother around?"

"Nope."

"Good. I'll go put her things up. What room?"

"Three."

Tobias turned and yanked the camera bag strap from her shoulder, then strode through the front door, heavy boots clomping across the wooden floorboards inside.

Lena had opened her mouth to say she was sorry he was missing his brother, but snapped it shut at his abrupt departure. "Why is he glad his brother isn't here?" she whispered to Lennard.

The corners of his eyes wrinkled with his easy smile. "Because those boys fight like titans. It's best for everyone that they spend as little time in each other's presence as possible."

"But Tobias said this was a favor for his brother." God, why was she being so nosey, and why did she even care?

"They're family," he said, as if the answer should've been obvious. "Don't matter if they don't like each other. A good man takes care of family when they need help. My regular bush-pilot just had his firstborn, and he's shacking up in Anchorage with his wife while the babe is new."

Lena smiled. "Good for him."

"Indeed. A baby is always a blessing, and a daddy should be there to help if he's able." Lennard jerked his chin. "You ready to meet the guides and get the grand tour of the place? You're the only one here for the next couple of days. Your boss booked you just right between guided tours. This season is a little slower."

"Why is that?" she asked, following him into a huge foyer and staring up at a massive antler chandelier above them.

"Hunting season starts in September for big game. That's our busy season. Right now is just sightseeing tours, fishing excursions, and guided camping trips. And pre-season scouting for big fancy magazine photographers," he added with a wink. "We subscribe to *Bucks and Backwoods*.

I knew your work from the credits at the bottoms of some of the pictures before your outfit even booked this place for you. You sure put a grin on this old man's face when I found out you were going to come take pictures of our bears. I wouldn't mind if you signed a couple of our in-house copies before you leave. The clients will get a kick out of it."

Lena grinned and said, "I'd be happy to."

Off the entrance was a great room with a grand stone hearth with a stuffed moose head over the cedar mantle. And under the dark leather couches in front of a big screen television was laid a bear-skin rug that had to be twice her height. The head was enormous, the mouth open in a menacing growl, and the gleaming teeth were longer than her fingers. "Holy shit," she said on a breath.

"Holy shit indeed, ma'am. You'll be in the thick of bears even bigger than that one."

There was an open kitchen and dining area on the other side, and around an island, eating what looked to be some sort of steaming soup, sat two men with their backs to them.

"Chance, Dalton, come meet Lena Rhodes."

The men, as different as night and day, one fair-haired with barely-there blond eyebrows and striking green eyes, and the other with tan skin, raven-black short hair and dark eyes, approached with friendly smiles.

"Chance Dawson," the blond said, shaking her hand.

"Dalton Dawson," the other introduced himself, giving her a good shake, too.

She liked the way they shook her hand. Usually, men in her industry gave her a limp handshake, or they turned her hand over, placing theirs on top of hers in a subtle play for dominance. None of these men had done that, though. It was all firm grips and friendly smiles. Good.

"Both of your last names are Dawson? Are you brothers?"

"Cousins," Chance explained. He shoved Dalton's head playfully and said, "We grew up together, and then Dalton followed me here. He just couldn't pry himself away from me."

"Shut up," Dalton muttered. He swung his gaze to Lena and said, "Our family is really close."

"Yeah," Chance murmured with a mischievous glint in his eyes. "Like a pack."

Dalton threw his cousin the strangest warning glance, then changed the subject. "You're the photographer Lennard won't stop yammerin' on about, aren't you?"

Heat flushed her cheeks, and she laughed. "Well, I haven't proven myself yet."

"What are you photographing?"

"Brown bear."

Dalton drew back like he'd been slapped. "Brown bear? You realize we are in the thick of the Kodiak Archipelago, don't you?"

She narrowed her eyes. "Yeah, so?"

"So Kodiak bears are the biggest, baddest, meanest bruins in the world. We'll be taking you out to the rivers for salmon season right now where grizzlies are desperately trying to build up their fat reserves for winter. That's no-man's land, and you're…well…a woman."

And there it was. "Damn, Dalton, and you gave such a good handshake, too."

Lennard was staring at the dark-haired guide like he'd lost his mind, and Chance was looking at her as if she was a mother wolverine about to bite the shit out of everyone.

"I was about to ask who you'd like to take you out there, but I have a feeling this dumbass just made your decision for you," Lennard grumbled.

Tobias strode from hallway to the front door with a polite half-smile and a wave. "Good luck with those bears," he said, which reminded her…

"I choose Jenner Silver."

"Ha!" Dalton crowed. "You think I'm bad? Jenner's ten times worse and grumpy to boot."

"Plus, he ain't here," Chance explained. "He's on a pre-season scout right now, and nobody knows when he'll return."

Lennard, however, was staring at her with a slight frown in his bushy gray brows. "That's not all true."

"He's not grumpy?" she asked hopefully.

"Oh, that part is one-hundred percent correct, but I know when he's returning. Any time now. He radioed in this morning. Got in a scuffle with a bear about thirty miles from here."

"Is he hurt?" she asked, worry unfurling in her chest. She didn't even know the man, but she'd been there when one of her co-workers got in a "scuffle" with a black bear, and it had left him disfigured.

"He'll be fine," Dalton grumbled. "That man has a hide tougher than jerky. I will say…you might not enjoy your trip as much—"

"Dalton," Lennard warned.

"No, let me say my piece. You were the one talking about how important it is to make Ms. Rhodes happy here, and you and I both know Jenner isn't capable of making a good impression on anyone." He swung his dark gaze to her. "If you want an enjoyable trip, you'd be better off with me or Chance. Or hell, even this old fart." He gestured to

Lennard. "Jenner's patience is about this thin," Dalton said, squishing his finger and thumb together, "and he's about as nice as a porcupine with hemorrhoids."

Tobias had stopped at the door, and now he spoke up. "She said she chooses Jenner. She wants the grizzlies, and you two dipshits will get her killed. Now shut the fuck up and give her the tour. Lena," he said, ducking his head in farewell, "hope you don't die." Then he turned on his heel and strode from the lodge, slamming the door behind him.

Lennard watched him leave with his cheeks puffed full of air, then he let out a long exhalation as he leveled his guides with a look. "Jenner's her guide. You two get back to eating while I give her the tour."

Grumbling, the two guides meandered back into the kitchen while Lennard explained how her trip would go. "I'll be cooking your meals while you stay here, and when you leave to find those bears, it'll be on horseback. Jenner will take care of your gear and pack your animal, as well as cook when you are roughing it."

"How long will we be out in the bush?"

"Depends. Jenner does things differently. If you were with Chance or Dalton, I'd say two days, maybe three. Jenner hunts until he gets his clients the experience they want, though. It's why he's hard to book. I never know when he's going to have an opening for a new tour. And you're probably wondering why I put up with that."

"It crossed my mind."

"Well, Jenner's the best damned registered Alaskan guide there is. Forget that he owns half this place. He's the real deal. His success rate with spotting, scouting, and bagging big game is off the charts. Ask anyone in any outfit around here. Jenner is a living legend. He's turned down many, many offers to join other lodges to guide for them. For some reason, I got lucky enough that he dug his heels in here when I was about to lose the place, and he put up a huge investment just to help me keep it. He's good, but those boys are right. He has no patience for anyone, and he's not a big talker, so best wrap your head around that before you go out so you aren't disappointed."

"Sir, I'm just here to photograph grizzlies, not to make friends or have campfire singalongs. I'm comfortable with quiet."

Lennard inhaled deeply and nodded his head. "I bet you are. You'd have to be to travel on your own like you do."

The remark wasn't meant to offend, but pain slashed through her middle. If Lennard knew why she traveled as much as she did, he wouldn't be looking at her with his bright blue eyes all full of respect. He'd think her weak for running from her demons. She liked the old man, though, and wouldn't blur his opinion by explaining why she preferred the quiet.

Likely, she and Jenner would get along just fine.

TWO

Chance and Dalton had relaxed around her almost immediately and were now sitting on the big couch of the great room with their feet on the table, beers in hand, as they watched sports re-runs while Lennard was cooking something delicious smelling over the stove in the kitchen.

"You sure you don't want us to turn the channel to a reality show or something?" Dalton asked through a grin. "Billion dollar weddings or a cat show or something."

Lena snorted at the tease and muttered, "Fuck you."

Chance laughed and turned up the volume to better hear the sports announcer while Lena curled her feet under her on the dark leather reclining chair and went back to sketching ideal shots she wanted to take. It was silly since she knew as well as anyone that when she was in the moment, shooting pictures, a shot never went according to plan. And sometimes a money shot was one she would've never imagined. But this, sketching and planning, was tradition before a big shoot. It settled her mind and her nerves and allowed her to focus on the task at hand more easily.

Biting her bottom lip, she frowned as she erased the odd angled eyes of the grizzly she'd drawn. Satisfied after drawing them back, she twisted in her comfortable chair and asked for the fifth time, "Lennard, are you sure you don't want any help in there. I really don't mind."

"Yeah, make me a sandwich," Dalton said through a teasing grin.

She smiled and rolled her wrist, lifting her middle finger with a flourish before she went back to sketching. The little crap-starter was just trying to get under her skin, but if she'd learned anything hanging around mostly men in her profession, it was that when the teasing started, it was a sign of acceptance.

"No, you relax Lena," Lennard called over his shoulder. "Usually I'm cooking for a lot more people, so this is an easy meal."

Lena smiled to herself and pulled a blanket from the arm of the chair. She was already showered for the night and in a pair of flannel pajama bottoms and a long-sleeved shirt. It was July, but it was cold at night in this high-ceiling lodge. Thankfully, Lennard had sent her an extensive list of clothing she would need for a guided tour, so she'd come prepared.

The front door blasted open, and a mountain of a man ducked under the frame. When his striking blue eyes landed on her, Lena froze. His dark hair was cut short on the sides, but he wore it longer on top, and his jaw was hidden by a beard as black as pitch, making the vivid sky-color of his eyes even brighter. His nose was straight and his jawline strong, his cheekbones sharp. He looked like some wild animal, the way he straightened his spine slowly until he was at his full imposing height. Lifting his chin, he looked down at where she sat in the chair and dragged his gaze to the sketchpad in her lap, then back to her eyes.

Holy hell, they didn't make them like this back home. Rugged, burly mountain man almost as tall as the bear skin rug under her chair, and oh Mylanta, the green sweater he wore was like a second skin, allowing her a peek at his defined chest and abs. He shrugged his arms until the open front of his jacket hid his body from her, and his eyes narrowed as if he didn't appreciate her attention.

"Jenner, meet your new client," Lennard said blandly from the kitchen.

Jenner jerked his gaze to Lennard and waited a few seconds too long with his response to be polite. "Where's the rest of them?"

"The rest of who?" Lena asked, pushing the blanket to the side and standing up to her full, not-so-imposing height.

"Your team."

She arched her eyebrows and shrugged. "No team."

Jenner gritted his teeth. "The men you've come with."

Dalton chuckled and sang low, "Here we go."

Lena stifled a curse. "No men, Mr. Silver. Just me."

"And what are you wanting to do? Please God tell me it's a fishing excursion."

"You can call it that. We'll be going to the rivers at least, but I'm here for the bears."

"Bears," Jenner repeated softly, eyes going hard as ice.

"Brown bears to be exact."

"They aren't in season. Sorry."

"Oh, I want to shoot them, but not with a gun. I'm a photographer."

Jenner let off a huffed, humorless laugh and shook his head. "Uh-uh. Hell no. Lennard, I'm not doing it."

"Now Jenner, she is an important client for us."

Jenner approached her slow but spoke to Lennard. "I don't care who the fuck she is. I'm not taking her out there.

Not to photograph grizzlies. You want to go fishing, you let me know. Otherwise, pick Chance or Dalton for your death wish."

"I was told you are the best."

Jenner came to a halt right in front of her. Damn, he was tall. She had to arch her neck all the way back just to meet his glare.

"Flattery won't get me to take you out there. This is my hard no."

"Why? I have experience. I've been shooting black bears for the past year."

"Black bears? Woman, those are fucking kittens compared to brown bears. Tell whoever sent you here that you're sorry to disappoint them, but you want to live. Go back to wherever you come from, live a long happy life taking pictures of pygmy donkeys and armadillos or whatever it is you need to photograph to get by, and enjoy the rest of your days not in the stomach of a fucking grizzly."

"Jenner," Lennard said in a steely voice. "This is Lena Rhodes."

"I still don't care who she is, old man. She isn't hunting grizzlies with a camera. I'm not doing it. I'm really not. Especially not when she's…"

"Finish it. Especially not when I'm what? A novice? A woman?"

Jenner clenched his teeth so hard a muscle jumped in his jaw. "Yeah, the last one." He turned on his heel and disappeared down the hallway.

She stood there, entirely stunned and completely infuriated at the ridiculous man. What was he complaining about? She wasn't some inexperienced photographer. She'd been shooting wildlife her entire five-year career, slowly working her way up until she was ready for this opportunity. Pygmy donkeys and armadillos. She wanted to choke him and slap him and kick him in his family jewels all at once.

She stomped after him, hands clenched at her sides lest she get an even bigger and less controllable urge for violence.

"I wouldn't," Dalton warned.

But hang it all, the magazine had paid an astronomical amount of money to get her in this position for grizzly money shots, and the guide she'd chosen was out on the excuse that she was a woman? Hell no.

There were several bedrooms down this hallway, and one of them was hers, so she took a chance and shoved the door with the number two painted onto it.

She'd guessed right because Jenner stood near a sink on the other side of the room, completely shirtless and peeling off a crimson-soaked bandage that wrapped around his torso. He turned around so fast, she could've sworn he blurred, and now his eyes were blazing a strange blue-brown color she'd never seen before.

"What happened?" she asked in shock, stumbling forward a step.

"Nothing," he rushed out, holding the loose end of the bandage he'd been removing.

She shut the door behind her, but he put a hand out. "No, don't come in."

"How long does it take to get a doctor out here?"

"A long ass time, but I don't need a doctor. Stop coming closer woman. Just…stay over there."

Ignoring him completely, she marched over to him and swatted his hand away from the loose wrapping. He sighed the most irritated sound she'd ever heard, but she gave exactly zero figs right now because he definitely looked like he was bleeding out. She unwrapped the stiff binding, mostly dried with his blood. Steeling herself on the last layer, she ghosted Jenner a glance. His chest was heaving as he looked down at her with some unfathomable expression. "You scared of blood, woman?" he asked in a deep, growly timbre.

Too many times to count, she'd relived the memory of her co-worker, Jason, mauled by a black bear and out in the woods where she spent hours staunching his blood flow until help could arrive. "No." She peeled off the last sticky layer that clung to his skin. He winced but didn't make a sound. Four long claw marks wrapped from his front around to his back, and what looked like puncture wounds had pierced his skin right under his arm. She shook her head and sighed. "I'm not scared of blood because I've seen this before. How did you get away?"

Jenner's lip lifted at one corner, and his eyes softened just before he looked away. No answer—fantastic. Still a dick then.

"This looks really bad. Why didn't you get Lennard and the others to help with first aid?"

"Because this is none of their damned business and besides, I heal fast."

"Stubborn and idiotic. Sa-weet."

A soft humming sound rumbled in his chest, but when she looked up at him, the sound stopped and his eyes sparked, daring her to ask what the hell that was about. She glared at him and tossed the bloody bandages in the trashcan by the sink. "Would you like me to disinfect it, or are you too stubborn to ask for my help?"

"Can you keep your mouth shut about the injury?"

Lena rolled her eyes. "Sure. If you want to die of infection or sepsis, that's your own choice."

Jenner snorted. "This is nothing."

On closer inspection of his skin, she believed him. Long healed silver scars covered most of his torso, so thin and light, she'd almost missed them. She wanted to ask him badly how he'd survived such injuries, but his eyes had closed down completely, and that ticking in his jaw was back. With a sigh, she yanked the first aid kit off the countertop and pulled it open, then picked and chose what she needed.

She bit a package of fresh bandages open with her teeth and grabbed a dark wash cloth from the bathroom. Carefully and wordlessly, she cleaned the half-dried gore from his body. It wasn't until she'd cleaned his wounds completely that she noticed the actual body she was working on. Thick with muscle, defined indentations between his pecs, eight-pack abs and those sexy strips of muscle delving into the low slung canvas pants he wore. His stomach flexed with every breath as he watched her. As she picked up the bottle of hydrogen peroxide, Lena swallowed hard and tried to focus on steadying her now shaking hands.

Just before she poured it over his injury, her palm cupped with a washrag underneath to catch any spillage, Jenner grabbed her trembling hand. His nostrils flared. Softly, he said, "You don't have to do this if you're scared."

"I'm not scared," she lied.

His eyes narrowed slightly as if he didn't believe her, but he let her hand go.

"This will hurt," she whispered sympathetically.

Jenner nodded once and held his breath, waiting.

Lena winced right along with him and rushed to clean the wounds so he would hurt as little as possible. And only when he was dressed in fresh bandages did she make her way to the bed and sit heavily on the mattress. Jenner's eyes followed her as he pulled a clean shirt carefully over his torso. "How did you learn to do that?"

"I told you. I have experience with black bears."

"You been clawed?"

She shook her head. "One of my friends was when we were out in the field."

"Did he live?"

She exhaled a shaky breath and swallowed down her nausea, then nodded. Barely, but she wasn't up for talking about Jason with him.

Jenner stared at her for a long time, hands on his hips and head cocked. His churning eyes said his mind was in a war over something she didn't understand, and at last, he muttered a curse. "What I said earlier about you being a woman. That's not it. That's not the reason I don't want to take you out there."

"Then what is it?"

Jenner looked entirely uncomfortable now, shifting his weight from side to side and looking anywhere but her. "You're on your period."

Lena felt slapped. Of all the millions of word combinations she could imagine coming from this confounding man's mouth, she would've never guessed he would have just called out her cycle. "Excuse me?"

Another one of those growly sounds came from him. "I can smell you bleeding, woman. The bears and the wolves will be able to smell it, too. It'll be like a fucking dinner bell. I'd planned on being out another week, but I don't take risks like that with injuries," he murmured, gesturing to his bandaged side. "Not with the bears we have out there. You think that black bear attack was bad? I'm telling you, your world is about to be rocked once you spend some time with the brown bears. I won't take you out until you stop bleeding."

Her heart was pounding against her ribcage so hard it ached. "You can smell me bleeding?"

"Don't get grossed out. I'm not. It's natural, but it's a risk. And since it'll just be us out in the bush with the monsters, I want to limit those risks. Do you understand?"

"Tomorrow," she said on a mortified breath. "I should be done bleeding tomorrow."

He nodded once and cleared his throat. "Then we'll leave the next morning."

"Okay." This was her cue to go because her cheeks were on fire right now. Ducking her head to hide her blush, she stood and bolted for the door to escape.

"Lena?"

She paused with her hand on the knob but didn't face him. "Yes?"

"This isn't about you being a woman, okay? I have a sister-in-law, Elyse, and she's as strong as any man I've ever met." Jenner swallowed audibly. "Thanks for doctoring me."

Lena nodded once, yanked the door open, and then closed it behind her with a firm *click*.

She let herself into her own room next door and locked the latch behind her. As she chugged shocked breath, she stared at the wall that stood between her and Jenner Silver.

What was this feeling pulsing through her? She'd never reacted to talking to a man like this. Dominant, growly hunting guide, all scarred and fearless and looking down at her with those vivid blue eyes in a way that made her blood burn for something she didn't understand. Lena clenched her shaking hands at her side.

Jenner Silver had just become as terrifying as the bears.

THREE

Jenner frowned sleepily in the mirror at the long, half-healed pink marks across his side. He couldn't be so careless around Lena again. He'd seen the fire in her eyes last night when he'd been harsh with her and should've known a spitfire like her would follow him into his room. It was the first time he'd been busted with an injury, and if it happened again, she would figure out he was healing way too fast. The grizzly in his middle made it possible to survive some brutal battle wounds, but that was his secret to keep, and if he had to guess, Lena was too observant for her own damned good. Of course, when he really thought about it, he had no reason to make that assumption other than she was a photographer and saw the world differently. He didn't know the woman, but his instincts were screaming to be careful around her.

With a growl, he pulled his shirt back down and threw away the bandages she'd dressed the claw marks with. He was done bleeding, and he didn't get infections. Never had and never would. That was the upside to this grizzly shifter gig. Almost everything else sucked. Being hungry all the time, trying to control a monster inside of him, stifling growls constantly, and hiding his changing eye color. But that wasn't the worst part. Hibernation was the bane of any bear shifter's existence. Six months in the winter, from October to April, consisted of him hiding deep in a den and sleeping the entire snowy season, and then in the warm months, he worked as a guide. Eat, work, sleep, repeat, year after year, and he'd been perfectly happy with that routine until Lena had given him that sexy blush last night. Spitfire she might be, but she was sensitive in ways that pulled at his protective instincts. And suddenly eating, sleeping, and working felt hollower than it did the day before.

Fuck, he couldn't do this. He couldn't afford to lose his head over a woman over the damned pink color in her cheeks. Sure, she was a stunner—dark hair, honey-colored eyes, tan skin, and pouty lips he wanted to bite. Even her pajamas were fucking adorable, flannel with tiny hearts on them, clinging to her curves and making it real hard to stand still when she was so close to him last night. Lena what's-her-face was the first woman he'd allowed into his room in…well…ever.

Jenner shoved his feet into his boots and sighed in irritation. Okay, he hadn't allowed her into his room, per say. More like she'd barged in unannounced and ignored him completely when he told her to leave, but for some reason, her gumption made her more interesting.

And his bear's interest in her wasn't good for anyone involved. He needed to stay neutral with her, distant even, because growing feelings for her was not only dangerous to the woman, it was a recipe for disaster with his bear when she left. He just had to get through the tour, let her take pictures of a few of the less violent, two-year-old grizzlies, and bring her back here. Then send her on her way, no feelings, no strings.

Jenner shoved his pant legs over the tops of his tied boots and nodded. Plan made, he could do this. Lena was just another woman. When his bear growled his disagreement inside of him, he swallowed the snarl back down. *Shut up, monster.*

Outside in the great room, breakfast was on. Lennard had gone all out with bacon, biscuits and gravy, scrambled eggs, and waffles. Waffles?

"Morning," he murmured to Lennard and the other guides. He forked a waffle and held it in the air. "You only bring out the waffle-maker on special occasions. What gives?"

Dalton and Chance were busy shoveling breakfast into their maws, but Lennard shoved a magazine across the wooden island countertop toward him. "I told you she was a big client, dumbass. You went off on one of the big-shot photographers for *Bucks and Backwoods*." He jammed his finger at the tiny white lettering in the bottom corner of a full page photograph of a black bear sow in a forest. There was a small amount of gray on her muzzle, but her eyes were forward and interested, and in the background was a small cub following behind her.

Photo Credit: Colleen Rhodes
Bucks and Backwoods Magazine, 2015

"Oh, shit," he murmured, pulling the magazine closer.

"Yep, and give me that waffle," Lennard gritted out, yanking the fork out of Jenner's hand. "You're in the doghouse, and dogs don't get my world-famous waffles."

He muttered on about how his grandma's recipe wasn't going to be wasted on ill-tempered tour guides who chased away big clients. Jenner stopped listening. Several pages of the magazine had been dog-eared, and each one had a picture that Colleen, aka Lena, had taken. She was good. Better than good. And Jenner remembered all these photos because he read *Bucks and Backwoods* from cover to cover every month when he had downtime between tours.

"Where is she?" he murmured. *Please say she hasn't left.*

Lennard jerked his chin toward the giant picture window in the great room behind Jenner. "Out there. Go tell her breakfast is on and apologize for being a dipshit while you're at it. The last thing we need is bad press in her magazine."

"Yeah, okay. I'll bring her in." Jenner walked out of the lodge, magazine still in his hand because he was feeling fifty percent bad for the way he talked to her last night and fifty percent dooped that she hadn't just come out and name-dropped herself.

She was near the river, knelt down, shooting a photograph. He should announce his presence because she definitely wouldn't hear his naturally quiet footsteps, but right now, she had him stunned. She wore a pair of jeans that clung to her curves and a V-neck sweater the color of late season blueberries that made it real easy for him to see the top part of her full breasts. But while his attention usually stopped at a woman's figure, his body's instant reaction to the rest of Lena shocked him to his bones. The early morning sunlight shone off her dark hair and drew his attention like a shiny lure in front of a fish. She'd put it up in some sort of black rubber band, high at the back of her head, and her ponytail cascaded to her shoulders in soft waves. The bottom few inches of her hair were lighter by a shade, a subtle auburn color in the saturated light, as though she'd paid someone to dye her hair that way. He hadn't noticed it in his dim room last night, but he liked it. Wanted to touch it just to see if it was as soft as it looked. And if his attention on anything other than those perfect tits of hers wasn't driving him insane enough, when she adjusted her position, the wide neck of her shirt exposed part of her collarbone near her neck. His favorite fucking part of a woman, and now his fingers were itching to touch her skin as well as her hair. *Lock it down, Silver.*

"What are you taking pictures of?" he asked as he approached.

She startled and stood so fast she fumbled with her camera and almost dropped it. "Oh, dear goodness, you scared me." She gripped her little picture-taker to her chest and looked him up and down. "How are you so quiet? You're the size of a barn."

37

Right now he was. If she saw him right out of hibernation, she wouldn't look so impressed. He'd been packing on weight and muscle for two full months already and was going to get even bigger as the warm season went on.

He lifted the magazine instead of answering. "Colleen Rhodes. Why didn't you tell me?"

"What, you mean between the yelling, growling, cussing, and bleeding you did last night? You didn't ask, and I don't go around telling people I work for a magazine. That's a dick move."

Huh. Fair enough. "I don't do this much, so bear with me."

"Do what?"

"Apologize."

Lena splayed her legs and locked her knees like she was bracing herself against a storm. "Okay, I'm ready."

"Well...that was it."

Lena pursed those pretty lips of hers and looked none too impressed with him. "That might be the worst apology I've ever heard. I'll help you out. Repeat after me. I'm sorry I was a peckerwood."

His inner bear balked against being told what to do, so he narrowed a glare at the woman. Five-foot-six with curves for days and that smart mouth on her, and why was the fire in her dark eyes turning him on so much right now? To hide his growing boner, Jenner bent down, picked up a flat pebble from the beach, and skipped it across the water. "I'm sorry," he muttered.

"Me, too."

Shocked, he jerked his gaze to hers just to see if she was joking, but her expression was completely serious. A smile cracked her face an instant before she lifted her camera to her eyes and snapped a picture of him.

Irritated, he gave her his back. "I don't like my picture taken. If I'm going to take you out tomorrow, that has to be part of the deal. Point that camera of yours at the wildlife, not at me."

"You feel like part of the wildlife," she murmured so low he would've missed it if he didn't have his heightened shifter senses.

Discomfort snaked in his gut as he looked at her over his shoulder. "What do you mean?" She couldn't find out what he was. Not ever. If she found out shifters existed, she could put his people in danger.

Lena cast him a quick glance, there and gone before she answered, "Because you feel like some wild thing, Mr.

Silver. All clawed up and big with those observant eyes. I bet you're right at home in the wilderness out here."

That pretty pink color tinged her cheeks again.

"This is a bad idea." He spun on his heel and left her on the bank of the river. "Breakfast is on."

"Wait, what's a bad idea?" she called.

"Us tracking bears together."

"But you're still going to take me, right?"

His chest rattled with another snarl as he thought of telling her no. What choice did he have, though? She was important to Silver Summit Outfitters and could put their lodge on the map with just a few nice words. She had major sway in the industry that directly impacted the annual income of his business. Sure, she was dangerous as hell, and his inner animal had never been more in jeopardy of being found out thanks to her seeing things others just put off as an odd quirk or strange habit. But if she wanted him as her guide, how could he say no?

She'd just called him a wild thing and nailed him right on the head. She was right. He was about as wild as they came, and now he was going to spend days with her, unable to escape her questions and stares. Fuck.

"Jenner! You're still taking me, aren't you?" she repeated.

Lennard stood on the porch with his arms crossed over his chest, tossing mind grenades his way with his pissed-off glare, and Jenner was completely trapped by circumstance.

"I don't have any choice in the matter," he barked over his shoulder.

When Lena's face dropped, Lennard smiled his approval, and Jenner wanted to shred a spruce tree with his bear claws just to hurt something.

He was some *wild thing*, huh?

Jenner pushed his way past Lennard and into the lodge, away from Lena's too-sharp eyes.

She had no idea.

FOUR

With her mouth hanging open, Lena watched Jenner disappear into the lodge. His change in mood had been immediate and utterly baffling. Was it because she'd called him a wild thing? Well, he was! Lena scanned the vast wilderness that surrounded the log mansion. Jenner was an outdoor guide who seemed to be completely comfortable out in the wild, scouting by himself, and he was offended? She'd meant it as a compliment.

Feeling off balance, she made her way past Lennard into the lodge. Jenner was stacking his plate high with waffles, his back to her. Lightly, she touched his elbow, but he lurched away like she'd burned him with a branding iron.

Stifling her hurt at his reaction, she murmured, "I'm sorry if I said something wrong."

As a response, she got a flash of those narrowed blue eyes and nothing more.

"Okay then."

Jenner grabbed a mug of steaming coffee and, with plate in hand, he strode from the lodge and out to the deck near the river. Dalton cleared his throat from the chair beside her, and Lena blinked hard to drag her gaze away from Jenner's retreat. When she looked down at the dark-headed man, he was grinning obnoxiously big.

"I have a question."

Turning to the empty plate on the counter, she began to fill it with the remaining food the boys had left. "Let's hear it."

"What are you still doing here?"

"Eating breakfast, numbnuts. It's the crack of dawn."

"No, not here in the kitchen. Why didn't Jenner take you out to brown bear country this morning?"

Resisting the urge to cast a look over her shoulder at the picture window where she would see Jenner eating his breakfast, she muttered, "Because of your no-period rule."

"What's that?"

Dumping syrup on her waffle, she answered without thinking. "The one where you won't take a woman out who's on her period, so I don't draw the bears in."

Chance gulped a bite and frowned down at his waffle, covered in bright red strawberry preserves. "Shit woman, seriously?"

Dalton sniffed the air near her, nostrils flaring. He nodded thoughtfully with his lips all pursed. "Huh. Makes sense."

"Okay, why do I get the feeling that is just something Jenner made up to stall now? And stop sniffing me." Lena sidled away from Dalton and made her way around the island to a pan of scrambled eggs.

"Would you like a heating pad?" Dalton asked innocently.

"Stop it."

"Or perhaps some ice cream and chick flicks?"

Chance had given up on his red waffles, but he was snickering now as Lennard gave them both an exhausted look. "Boys, this isn't appropriate talk with one of our clients. I apologize for their asshattery, Lena. You have my permission to slap them if they get too cheeky."

"Oh, I don't slap, Lennard," she said through a grin. "I'm more of a punch and stab kinda gal." She poured herself a mug of coffee and made her way to the door. "Chance, you enjoy those waffles now."

The man groaned, Lennard laughed, and right before she walked out the front door, Lena looked behind her to see Dalton shove a spoonful of strawberries in his cousin's face.

She held in her laugh until the door was firmly closed behind her so they wouldn't hear. Those men did not need any encouragement from her.

At the top of the porch stairs, Lena hesitated. Jenner seemed to want to be alone, but she felt weird eating breakfast on the porch, basically staring at him as he ate near the river. His sexy, wide-as-a-canyon shoulders would be blocking half the danged scenery from here.

His back went tense long before she reached him, as if he heard her coming all the way from the house, which was impossible, of course.

She cleared her throat as she stood next to a lounge chair and asked, "Is anyone sitting here?"

He cast her a wary glance, then took a long pull of his coffee and returned his attention to the gentle rapids in front of them.

"That was a joke," she muttered, sitting down beside him. She ate in silence for a while before she said, "I forgot to ask how your side is doing this morning. Do you want me to re-do the bandages later?"

"Woman, let me be. It's not a good idea for you to be touching me anymore."

"Why not?" she asked as anger snapped through her. "Am I disgusting? Does my touch make your skin crawl? I was trying to help, you megadick. Not traumatize you." She clutched her plate to her middle and went to stand, but Jenner's hand was suddenly on her wrist. She hadn't even seen him move from his relaxed position on the chair, but instantly, he was pulling her back down. She gasped as her backside hit the cushion. Jenner Silver was as fast as a snake strike.

"You are the opposite of disgusting, and I'm not trying to piss you off, but we aren't friends, Lena. I'm your guide. Nothing more, and last night was too..."

"Intimate?"

"Yeah, okay? It was too fucking intimate. I'm a professional. This is where I work and where I live, and you came in here and..."

She was arching her eyebrows so high, her forehead wrinkles hurt. "And what?"

He relaxed back onto his chair and gritted his teeth so hard the muscles in his jaw clenched. Jenner sighed. "It's just best if we keep our distance, all right? You doing shit like dressing my injuries complicates feelings."

Lena gasped, then pursed her lips to hide a smile that was trying to take over her face. Feelings? Now she knew she wasn't the only one who felt the flaming hot sparks between them.

She kept her eyes directed carefully at the river, but in her peripheral vision, Jenner was staring at her. "What?" he asked.

"What what?"

"What are you smiling about?"

She arched her gaze to him. "Complicates my feelings or your feelings?"

His eyes narrowed to suspicious little slits. "Does it matter?"

To avoid the obvious answer that was bouncing around in her giddy mind right now, she shoveled a huge bite of waffle into her mouth hole and grinned as she chewed.

"You eat like an anaconda," he muttered.

She shrugged, unoffended. So she was a messy eater. There were worse insults out there.

But now Jenner was staring at the southern half of her face with a dazed look in his bright eyes. "You have syrup on your lips."

Oh, she knew she did because she could feel it. She wiped the wrong side just to annoy him. "Bether?" she asked around her food.

"Not at all."

She gulped her food down and took a finger-full of whip cream from the side of her plate, then smeared it on the corner of her lip. "Better now?"

Jenner growled and shook his head like she was ridiculous, but she could see it now. There was a slight lift to the corner of his grumpy mouth. He gripped her chair and pulled it across the deck toward him until her knees were encased between his. With a challenging look in his eyes, he wiped his thumb gently over the sugary mess she'd made, then he drew his thumb into his mouth and sucked it off.

Lena's smile fell from her face, and her heart stopped as he lowered that brilliant gaze to her lips again. He was only inches away, and now she couldn't breathe. He leaned forward, so near she could feel his warmth as he ran his big hands up her legs. Squeezing gently at the tops of her thighs, he eased forward until his lips were at her ear. "It'll complicate *your* feelings, Lena."

Then he stood and carried his empty plate and coffee mug toward the lodge, leaving her staring after him and feeling utterly touched. Body touched, heart touched, soul touched, and now her breath came back ragged.

Jenner Silver was a complete stranger, but she'd never wanted to be kissed by a man so badly.

And from the swell of his cheeks that said he was smiling as he walked away, Jenner knew it, too.

****

Dalton Dawson was a flirt. Lena had spent the day fishing and hiking the nearby trails with the Dawson cousins because Jenner had done his damndest to avoid her. Now it was late in the evening, and Dalton had taken on the personal challenge of teaching Lena how to tie flies so when she returned, she could fly-fish with her own lures. At least, that's what he'd told her, but right now, he was leaning over her shoulder from behind, arms wrapped around her, fingers on hers as he showed her the knots.

Lena had swatted him away about a dozen times today, but at this point, it was downright funny, and she was pretty sure he was paying attention to her because he found her amusing and easy to tease. He reminded her of Adam. That thought washed sadness and joy through her all at once. She closed her eyes and smiled at the memory of his face. Adam had been her best friend growing up, and Dalton's fun-loving personality had given her a precious moment. It had been a long time since thoughts of Adam had made her happy.

"Ow," she muttered as she stared down at the swelling red dot on her thumb where the tiny hook had pricked her.

"Well, you have to pay attention, girl. Stop falling in love with me and focus," Dalton teased.

"Aw, piss off," she said, shoving him with a laugh. "I'm married."

Dalton jolted upward, spine straight as a rod, and Chance dropped the magazine he was reading from the leather couch near them. "You are?"

"To my work."

"Ha!" Chance said, jamming a finger at Dalton. "You should see your face right now."

Jenner strode through the front door and halted when his eyes landed on her. He dragged that sexy blue-flame gaze to Dalton and narrowed his eyes.

"He's aliiiive," Chance sang in a monster voice.

Something unfathomable sparked in the air between Jenner and Dalton for just an instant before the giant strode into the kitchen with his boots echoing across the wooden floors. "I've been packing."

"I think she should ride Hatchet," Dalton said, the tease melting from his voice.

"She'll be fine on Gunner."

"Gunner's too wild," Dalton argued.

"Uh, I'm experienced with horses," she said, frowning her disapproval at Dalton. "This isn't my first trail ride."

Dalton crossed his arms over his chest. "Gunner's young, and he's only been doing this two seasons."

"My tour, my choice. She'll be fine," Jenner gritted out, his back to them as he pulled the refrigerator door open.

"Yeah, but—"

"Careful, dog," Jenner murmured low, twisting to give Dalton a lethal look over his shoulder. "Hatchet runs at the first scent of bears. Gunner will get her where we need to go. She can handle him."

Dog? Lena was glad Jenner had more faith in her abilities than Dalton did, but the name he'd called him didn't make any sense. She didn't know whether to thank Jenner for sticking up for her or reprimand him for being rude to the guide gone rigid beside her. Best not to do either because from the way Dalton huffed a humorless laugh and met Jenner's terrifying gaze, she didn't understand the dynamics here.

"Dalton," Chance said, warning in his deep timbre. "Back off this one. Jenner's right."

Something heavy was in the air, pressing against her shoulders, lifting the fine hairs on her body. There was another moment of silence before Dalton dropped his gaze and nodded slightly. He ghosted her a glance, but his eyes looked strange. They looked lighter, more caramel than dark chocolate, and she blinked hard to clear her vision. But when she opened her eyes again, he was already striding toward the hallway.

"Night," he called behind him. And then his door shut a little too soundly.

She opened her mouth to ask what had just happened, but Jenner beat her to it. "You hungry?" he asked gruffly. "I'm making a grilled cheese. I can make one for you while I'm at it."

"And me," Chance said, turning the page of his magazine and leaning back into the couch with his feet propped up on the table, like Jenner and Dalton having dominance battles was a daily occurrence.

"Uh, sure. I'll take one, too." Hell no, she wasn't going to turn down a sexy-as-hell man cooking for her. Even if he was just being polite.

Lena set her half-finished fly on the table and trotted into the kitchen, slipping and sliding across the polished floors in her warm socks. "Where's Lennard?" she asked as Jenner shoved a loaf of bread toward her.

"Cut us some slices, will you? Lennard's out with the horses. He's a freak about getting everything just right with the packing the day before a tour. In the hunting season, he's even worse. I keep thinking one of these years he'll trust us to handle everything, but he goes over and over the packing three times at least."

"Does he ever find anything wrong with the way you pack?"

"No," Chance called from the great room. Another magazine page sounded. "He's just a control freak."

"Yeah, but his diligence is why this place thrived for so long," Jenner murmured distractedly.

She pulled a knife from a block on the countertop and smiled privately. Lennard had told her about Jenner turning down offers from other outfitters just to invest his money here and dig his heels in. She respected him more for giving Lennard the credit instead of bragging about his own importance. Jenner was a loyal man, and when his elbow bumped hers as he worked beside her, a strange fluttering feeling filled her middle.

When she'd imagined a grilled cheese dinner, she hadn't thought it would be so grand. Jenner cooked lemon pepper asparagus in a pan while she chopped a colorful fruit salad, and the grilled cheeses he made were the fanciest she'd ever seen. Three types of cheeses were melted right into the middle of butter-toasted French bread with the perfect amount of squish and crunch. Jenner left a trio of filled plates on the counter, and as they were sitting down at the giant twelve-seater dining table with the wagon wheel chandelier above them lighting the room, Dalton appeared to tuck into their meal with them.

"Sorry," he murmured to Jenner as he sat across the table from her.

Jenner jerked his chin dismissively from the seat right next to Lena. "Don't worry about it."

The tension in the air dissipated almost immediately, and Chance passed out cold beers. And bless that man, he didn't even joke about a fruity cocktail for her as he popped the cap off and handed one over.

"To a successful trip," Dalton toasted, holding his beer up. He'd said it to everyone, but his eyes were steady on Jenner.

Lennard walked in right as they tinked the glass bottles, then joined them with his own plate and frothy drink. Conversation was easy after that, and the joking and teasing commenced, much to Lena's relief. She hated worrying that any of the earlier tension had been because of her. Beside her, Jenner ate four sandwiches to her one, but she supposed a man his size needed a lot of calories to sustain himself. And when she finished her last bite and pushed her plate away by inches, Jenner leaned back in his chair, his arm hooked on the ladder back of her seat.

She wanted to think he was being possessive, but from his little duck-and-run this morning, he likely was relaxed and had accepted her as one of the guys. This is how it happened with any man she had found interesting since Adam. The friend-zone swallowed her up quickly out in the field. Something about her made her great surrogate sister material, but little more. And for some reason, watching Jenner smile at something Chance had said, that thought made her really sad this time. She was attracted to him, but it was more than that. The more she got to know about the quiet giant of a man, the more she wanted to know, and the more she respected him. But he saw her as a little buddy at most, and there was tragedy in that.

"Lena," Dalton said, looking troubled. "Did you hear me?"

"Huh?" she said, blinking rapidly and ripping her gaze away from Jenner.

"I asked how you got into wildlife photography."

"Oh, right. Sorry. Uh, I studied for it in college. I've been obsessed with photography since I was little and my mom got me this—" She laughed as heat flooded her cheeks. "Too much information."

"No, tell us," Lennard said, leaning forward on his elbows on the other side of Dalton.

"Okay. My mom bought me this Polaroid camera when I was a kid, and I fell in love with taking pictures of things I thought people missed in the everyday."

"Like what?" Chance asked.

She puffed air out of her cheeks and frowned, trying to recall some of her early photographs. "Like my mom's face when my dad brought her flowers. My sisters when they were actually getting along, playing in a sandbox." She swallowed hard and admitted low, "How beautiful and heartbroken my mom looked at my dad's funeral. That's weird, I know. But for me, it helped me deal with what was happening. I could see someone else's grief, and it was real and moving, and I didn't feel alone with my own heartache when I captured those moments that weren't the brave-face kind. I almost ran us broke with the refills for that old Polaroid camera, so when I was able, I saved up and bought a film camera. I love animals, so I volunteered at a local zoo every summer, mostly running the youth programs, but I would bring my camera along and take pictures of the animals in their cages. But that made me sad, seeing them all cooped up, and every picture had some kind of fencing in it, no matter what angle I shot, so when I started taking my college classes for photography, I took animal sciences, behavior, and husbandry for electives so that I could work toward...well...this. I got lucky and landed an internship at *Bucks and Backwoods* right when they started up, and now I'm here, shooting Alaskan brown bears."

"Lucky you," Chance said with a snort.

"I am. I beat out some of the best photographers in the company to come here. This is my shot at having one of those careers I only dreamed of. All of my hard work has led me to this trip. Alaska has been a dream of mine since I was a kid."

"Is this your first time here?" Dalton asked.

"My very first time."

"Alaska virgin," Dalton said through an obnoxious grin.

Lena rolled her eyes and sighed. If he knew how accurate his name calling was, he wouldn't ever let up on teasing her, so she just laughed it off and stood, empty plate in hand. "Storytime's over, boys. I'm beat."

Jenner pulled the chair back to allow her out, and she whispered, "Thank you," at his unexpected gentlemanly gesture.

Stomach churning with emotion—nostalgia for her journey here, sadness remembering Dad's funeral, and the strange tickling sensation in her middle that Jenner conjured—she rinsed her dish and waved goodnight to the men all sitting quietly around the dining table.

It wasn't until after she'd showered and was laying in bed, sketching in her notebook, that a soft knock sounded at her door. Only when she opened it, the man standing there wasn't the one she'd hoped for. It was Dalton, looking uncomfortable and unsure of himself.

"I wanted to say something, but I'll sound like a total dick, and you'll tell me it's none of my business, but I don't want to spend the next week thinking about you out there without warning you."

"Okay," she murmured, baffled.

He jerked his head toward Jenner's room and lowered his voice to a whisper. "Be careful with that one, Lena. He's a good man. The best. But he's not right for any woman. He can't keep one, you understand?"

Pissed that he was warning her off Jenner, she asked, "And you are the right kind of man for a woman, right?"

"No, I didn't say that. None of us are. We'd be worthless as mates—" Dalton dropped his gaze to the hem of her flannel pajama pants. "What I'm saying is, don't give your heart to someone who can't keep it safe." He gave her a sad smile, then without another word, turned and strode off toward his room at the entrance of the hallway.

His door clicked closed as she stood halfway in the hall, baffled on what had just happened. She frowned at Jenner's door and wondered just what she'd gotten herself into, choosing him as a guide.

Dalton's words hadn't sounded like the whispered deception of a jealous man.

They'd sounded like an honest warning.

FIVE

Great hairy balls, it was early. Jenner had knocked on her door at five in the morning and whispered for her to get ready. He was all ready to go, from his newly-shaven jaw to his forest green thermal sweater that clung to his sexy torso like a plastic bag with all the air sucked out. He had a backpack thrown over his shoulder and smelled of mint toothpaste.

She, on the other hand, took one look at herself in the mirror and laughed. How had he kept a straight face while he talked to her at the door? Her hair was naturally curly and had dried like she'd stuck a fork in a socket. In her haste to answer the door, she hadn't put her bra on, and both nipples were drawn up like beads against her sleep shirt. Fantastic.

She dressed quickly, brushed her teeth, and tamed her beastly hair with a curling iron, then pulled it back into a ponytail. Then she shouldered her heavy pack and made her way quietly through the dim lodge to the kitchen where Jenner was currently working on something over the countertop. Buttered biscuits from the smell, and when she sidled around the kitchen island, she could make out the grape jelly he was smearing onto seven or eight of them in a row.

"Breakfast for days?" she joked, fully aware of his appetite. When she picked up a half and bit into it, he gave a teasing growl.

"Woman, I don't know what you think you're doing, but these are all for me. Get your own."

"No," she said around the bite. "Lennard said my trail guide is in charge of all my meals."

"On the trail."

She picked up the other half and licked it before he could stop her, and now he was stifling that sexy smile. With a wicked grin, she set her pack down and hopped up on the counter beside where he was sweetening his plethora of carbohydrates.

He didn't move over as she'd expected him to when she sat close enough that his arm bumped her leg as he worked. Instead, Jenner seemed content to stay right where he was, watching her occasionally with an odd look in his dancing eyes as she ate his biscuit.

"You have ridden horses before, right?" he asked.

"Oh, millions of them."

"Be serious, woman. Your life depends on it."

She licked a smear of jelly off her thumb and offered him a pointed look. "I used to take lessons."

"Western or English."

Sarcastically, she answered, "Sidesaddle, like dainty ladies did in the olden days."

Jenner growled a low, humming sound, but he didn't look mad. "Okay, I get it. You can ride a horse. Dalton just got me thinking last night."

"That I was more helpless than I actually am?"

"I know you aren't helpless."

"How do you know, stranger?"

He made a ticking noise behind his teeth and twitched his head. "You don't seem the type. You remind me of my sister-in-law. Brave as shit but headstrong, so I just want to make sure you can handle the horse I give you."

"Gunner and I will be the best of friends."

"Mmm," he grunted noncommittally.

Dawn had brightened the horizon by the time Jenner carried her pack out toward the corral with her following directly. Even though it was July, nights were nippy, so she zipped her jacket up to her chin and jogged to catch up to

Jenner's ridiculously long strides, holding her camera that hung from her neck steady as she went. He nearly had her camera equipment tied to a bored-looking bay packhorse by the time she made it to where the lead horses were secured to a fence.

Gunner, as it turned out, was a dark chocolate-colored horse with no white markings at all, and a long, wavy mane the same color as the rest of his body. He was also a head-tosser as Jenner checked his saddle bags.

"What the hell is this?" Lena asked as she jammed her finger at a rifle secured against the saddle.

"Protection."

"But I said—"

Jenner rounded on her. "There's no room for that hippy dippy shit out here, Lena. We aren't hunting bears. The rifles are for protection, and that's all, but if you go out there without a defensive strategy, you're as good as dead. It's my job to protect you, and I'm not taking you out there unarmed. This," he said, slapping the leather rifle sheath, "is non-negotiable. Please tell me you know how to fire one."

Lena gritted her teeth and crossed her arms over her chest in rebellion.

"Answer me now, woman, or I swear we'll put off your pictures another day to target practice and learn this weapon."

With a pissed-off sigh, she said, "The gun is a thirty aught six and yes, I can handle the recoil."

"Good. Safety?"

"It's the small button on top of the rifle, over the trigger."

"Stance?"

She lifted her hands as if she cradled an imaginary rifle and splayed her legs to the side, still glaring at him.

"Okay." Jenner turned toward his own horse, a dapple gray whose attention was already on the woods, and who was currently stomping impatiently. Jenner spun around just before he hoisted himself into the saddle. "One last question. Where did you learn to shoot?"

"My dad." She hadn't meant for the words to sound like heartbreak on her lips, but there it was.

Some deep emotion slashed across Jenner's eyes for just a moment before it was gone and he looked stoic once again. "Very good."

She swung herself over Gunner's back and twisted to look at the packhorse that was tied to the saddle.

"If you need to run and drop weight quick," Jenner explained, pointing to the rope, "you drop that."

"What about the packhorse?"

"He'll stand a better chance of getting away if he isn't trailing you."

"Right."

"Come on," Jenner said low, kicking his skittering horse and pulling on the rope of his own following packhorse.

Gunner pranced under her, tossing his head as he blasted a snort in the early morning air, but he followed Jenner's packhorse without too much prompting, and the patient bay behind her didn't need any encouragement. He followed Gunner easily.

The hours directly following sunrise and directly preceding sunset were what Lena called the magic hours. Bar cloudy days, the lighting was always best during those times, and as the sun rose, she was stunned at how beautiful the woods here were. She'd been to some of the most breathtaking places in the world on her quest for photographs for *Bucks and Backwoods*, but this moment right here had to be one of the most profound. Gray and yellow streaked sky, snow-capped mountains, air so crisp and fresh it nearly burned her lungs, and vegetation so lush, the vibrant green was almost hard to look at for too long.

Birds called back and forth, and insects buzzed a constant song. The quiet clomping of the horses' hooves and swishing of their tails lulled her into a comfortable calm.

And all the while, she was adjusting her aperture and shutter speed, clicking away to capture these witching hours with her camera.

Jenner had said he didn't want her taking pictures of him, but she couldn't help herself. He was too beautiful not to photograph. The way he sat straight in the saddle, ear toward every forest noise. The way he cast a glance behind him at his packhorse as he urged it faster. The way his eyes looked when he scanned the woods. A haunted hunter ready for anything and missing nothing.

She shouldn't feel safe riding ever closer to the brown bears, but with Jenner, unexplainably, she did.

The trail they road thinned to nothing in the middle of a meadow, waving like an ocean current with tall wild grasses and occasional blue flowers. Here, Jenner stopped. His attention was to their left, and she could see his nostrils flare, as if he was scenting the air. Wild thing, indeed. She sniffed but didn't smell anything other than rich earth, pine sap, and horse crap, thanks to Jenner's upwind packhorse taking advantage of their stop to squeeze out a pile of meadow muffins.

Jenner turned in his saddle. "Are you only here to photograph brown bears?" he asked quietly.

"Brown bears top the list, but I wouldn't mind caribou, porcupine, ptarmigan, moose, waterfowl, wolves, black bears—"

"Okay, I got it. All animals."

She smiled brightly. "Yep."

He shook his head as he turned back around, but not before she saw the amusement on his face. And God, his distracted smile was beautiful. She wished she could've gotten a picture so she could look at it later when he wasn't around.

Jenner kicked his horse toward a grove of young trees and dismounted without a word, so she followed suit. He tied their lead horses to a low hanging branch and pulled her to him, so close she had to rest her hands on his chest to fight the urge to hug his waist. In her ear, he whispered, "Get your equipment. Long range shit if you have it."

"Okay," she said on a breath. His smooth jaw brushed her cheek as he pulled away. And while she clicked her long-range lens to her camera and pulled out a tripod, Jenner busied himself with loading a rifle. Bears? Her hands started shaking. This was it. She would finally see an Alaskan brown bear. Her middle became a warzone of excitement and terror while adrenaline dumped into her veins, making it feel like she was floating as she hiked after Jenner through the thick brush.

When the sound of splashing touched her ears, Jenner crouched and eventually lay down on the pine needle-blanketed ground. Slowly, quietly, they moved forward toward a tall wall of marsh grass, and when he carefully pulled the barrier aside, she had to swallow a gasp of excitement before she scared the animals off. It was a moose, standing belly-high in a pond, and behind her was a newborn baby, still wobbly but splashing with one hoof in the shallows.

When she turned to grace Jenner with a grateful look, he had moved closer to her and was staring at the smile on her lips with the most peculiar expression on his face. Hunger?

Now her nerves were out of control, and Jenner was the cause of it. Desperate to steady her trembling hands, Lena dragged her attention back to the animals. Jenner hid her actions by letting the grass fall gently back into place, and slowly, she set up her tripod on the shortest setting. When she was ready, he pushed it aside again. Her first shot brought a big old grin to her face. Momma moose was broadside, staring directly at them with a long strand of deep green pond grass hanging from her dripping lips, and the baby was mid-splash behind her. A money shot, and the perfect way to start this trip. *Bucks and Backwoods* was getting low on moose shots, and she was about to pump up their photo options for future issues. And not just with distant, hurried shots. Jenner had got her in extremely close with a long range lens, and momma moose was a fucking supermodel. Morning sun bouncing off her clean coat, ears erect and interested, she kept freezing to listen for danger, giving Lena shot after shot of un-blurred photographic gold. God, she couldn't wait to look at these pictures later because every one she reviewed between shots made her heart stutter. What an incredible, magnificent, gigantic, graceful animal, and her baby was adorable with personality for miles. And when the moose moved from the pond, Jenner brushed her waist lightly and gestured for her to follow him. Slowly, silently, they stalked the moose and set up again in the brush to take more shots of the pair drying off in the shade of a Western Hemlock tree. She even got shots of the mother nuzzling the baby's face and of the little one nursing.

Lena had taken classes on animal behavior for every species she would potentially come into contact with, and she knew just how dangerous Moose could be, especially mothers, but here, in the cover of the brush, she was astounded by the moment Jenner had secured for her.

Jenner Silver was good. He was real good.

The animals meandered off slowly, but he didn't make a move to leave. As they disappeared into the woods completely, Jenner turned to her from where he lay on his stomach beside her, and said, "Lena, I'm sorry about your dad."

She jerked the camera as she began to remove it from the small tripod and accidentally took a picture of the ground. "What?"

"You talked about your dad's funeral last night and how he taught you to shoot. Your voice sounds sad when you mention him, and I'm sorry for it. Sorry he's gone. Sorry you hurt."

For a minute, she couldn't find her words, nor could she push them past her tightening throat if she had, but at last, she swallowed hard and rested her cheek on her crossed arms. The sunlight was throwing gold speckles across his cheeks and one right against his eye, making it look fiercely beautiful. "Did you lose your dad?"

His eyes tightened as he huffed a soft breath. "This isn't about me. Let's go."

He made to stand up, but Lena clutched onto his wrist and kept him beside her. "What is your problem?"

His eyes empty, he shrugged and whispered, "I don't have a problem."

"You do!" she whisper-screamed. "One minute you're nice to me, and the next you're cold, and I can't keep up with your changing moods, Jenner. And furthermore—"

Jenner's lips crashed onto hers. Utterly shocked, Lena reared back and slapped him. The air sparked between them as they glared each other down, but Jenner had started a storm in her middle, churning and unavoidable, and before she could stop herself, she kissed him back. Hard. Jenner's hands were fire against her skin as he rucked up her shirt and rolled on top of her. His lips moved against hers, relentless and overbearing, and he used his teeth when he sucked on her bottom lip. Angry, turned on, and out of control, she bit his lip hard, and a rattling sound filled his chest. Wild thing.

He moved over her gracefully as he grabbed the back of her neck and pushed his tongue past her lips, and holy fuck, she could taste him now. He even tasted feral. A helpless moan left her as she rolled her hips against him. He lowered his mouth to the tripping pulse at her neck, shoved her knees farther apart, and ground his thick erection against her sex.

"Oooh, that feels good," she murmured, eyes rolling back in her head. This right here was what it felt like to lose her mind.

Jenner was like a star, too hot, too fast, and she was being burned up by him. But for some reason, she couldn't find a damned thing wrong with that right now. It had been so long since she'd wanted a man this badly. No, scratch that. She arched her back and sighed as he rocked his hips against hers again. She'd never wanted anyone like this. Was it rushing? Hell yes, and Jenner wasn't a man to give her heart to, but maybe if she could just forget about everything for a while, just let go, then perhaps she could find herself again in the aftermath. Aftermath? Ha. Jenner was a tornado that likely destroyed everything in his wake. If she did this with him, she faced destruction, but if she didn't…it felt like destruction that way, too.

His lips were back on hers, his breath quick as though he was just as lost in this as she was. When his warm hand pressed under her bra, cupping her full breast, she lost all reason. And if he didn't stop rubbing his giant dick against her jeans, she was going to come right here and now.

She reached under his shirt and clawed a long rake down his back with her nails, and Jenner arched his neck back. He reared up and pulled his shirt over his head, then tossed it into the grass beside them. The silver scars were stark against his tanned skin, and the new claw marks were red, raw, and un-bandaged. He was killing her with how fucking sexy he was.

"Claw me again." His eyes looked darker now. Maybe lust did that to him, or perhaps the mid-day, saturated sunlight behind him was to blame. Either way, she didn't care about anything right now other than the friction he was building between her legs and that sexy noise in his throat.

She obeyed, dragging her nails down his back again as he kissed her breathless. She ran her hands over the strips of muscles at his hips and reached down the front of his pants. The second she brushed the head of his shaft, a deep shiver took Jenner's shoulders. She'd done that, affected his body so easily. Feeling bold, she reached farther inside his pants and pulled a slow stroke of him.

"Fffuck," he murmured in a shaking voice as he rolled his hips against her hand.

And when she looked up to meet his gaze again, she could see it. The wildness, the abandon, the dazed look that said he was rutting and desperate for her.

"Jenner," she whispered, his name tinged with desperation from her lips. "Touch me."

There was a moment between them—just an instant— before Jenner leaned down, kissed her so hard she could feel his teeth against her swollen lips, then flipped her over like she weighed nothing.

Baffled on how she'd gotten on her hands and knees, she gasped as he unbuttoned the snap on her jeans and ripped her zipper downward. He reached into the front of her panties and as he dragged a finger against her clit, the sound rattling his chest turned guttural. It wasn't until he'd yanked her pants halfway down that she realized what he meant to do. He was going to take her from behind like some wild animal, but this wasn't the way it was supposed to be.

"Jenner," she panted out. "Not like this. Not for my first time."

Jenner jolted to a stop, one hand against the wetness he'd created between her legs, the other on the waist of her jeans. "What?"

Her arms were shaking now as the adrenaline in her pounding blood did something strange to her body. It softened the muscles and made it hard to hold herself upright. "I want it differently for my first time."

"Our first time," he said in a strange voice.

Lena swallowed hard and looked over her shoulder. "No, I mean, it's my first time to do this."

"With anyone?" His eyes went wide and horrified, and his expression hurt like a slap against her skin.

Unable to speak, she nodded.

Jenner ripped his hands away from her and crawled backward, as if he couldn't escape her fast enough. "You're a virgin?"

Tears stung her eyes now at how mortified he looked. Slowly, she sat back on her folded legs and pulled up her jeans. Lips pursed, she nodded again with her back to him.

"Fuck, Lena. We almost…I almost…I could've hurt you!" His voice snapped with anger, and she hunched her shoulders against it. "You should've been upfront with me."

"What are you talking about?" she cried in fury. "It's not something I talk about with everyone, Jenner! And I didn't know we were going to fool around. How could I have known? You like me one minute and reprimand me the next."

Jenner stood and ran his hands through his hair. "Are you waiting?"

"For what? Marriage?"

"Yeah! Because I'm telling you right now, I'm not even good to date."

"Yeah, everyone keeps telling me that, Jenner."

"What?"

"Dalton said the same thing, and I'm pretty fucking sick of not being trusted to make up my own mind who I want to

75

spend time with. And no, the idea wasn't to wait until marriage." She blasted upward and jammed her foot against the ground at the fact that Jenner was really going to pull this admission from her right now when she was pissed. "I was already married once."

Jenner drew backward like she'd socked him across the jaw. "You were married?" Now he was yelling in earnest, and the sheer volume of his voice stung her ears. "That doesn't even make any sense. How can you be a virgin if you were married?"

"Because it wasn't like that! I'm not waiting to have sex on purpose, you asshole. I just haven't found anyone I wanted to be intimate with since Adam died!" A pathetic sob clawed its way up her throat, and mortified, she grabbed her camera, tripod still attached, and half-jogged toward where the horses were tied. She had to get away from him—as far away as possible before she melted down completely— because nothing was more unacceptable in her life right now than crying in front of Jenner Ice-Heart Silver.

Gunner snorted and stomped his foot as she approached, but she didn't care. He was about to get snuggled because she needed that. She wrapped her arms around his neck and ignored that he bopped her in the back with a well-placed head toss. She cried against his coat until it was damp and his neck was spotted with dark spots, almost black against the rest of his dark coloring.

"What are you doing?" Jenner asked quietly from behind her.

Feeling puny, Lena muttered, "Nothing you would understand."

Jenner sighed. "Gunner's trying to bite you."

With a growl, she released the horse from her affection and stumbled toward the packhorse who looked utterly comatose. She was almost offended that the old horse hadn't bothered to wake up for her sob-fest. The silence as she packed her camera lens and tripod was only punctuated with her sniffles as she studiously ignored the grumpy Sasquatch she could feel watching her. "I need a minute." Stupid voice as it trembled.

She stomped off into the trees, and when she was good and alone, she slid her back down the rough bark of a pine and drew her knees to her chest. How dare he? No one had affected her so completely or made her feel so pitiful in all her life. She wasn't a ten, but she surely wasn't a two, and Jenner had looked at her like she was disgusting. All because she was a virgin? Yeah, she got it. Twenty-six was old to not have been with a man, but it wasn't like she'd planned this.

When she looked up and rested her head against the tree, Jenner was standing there, hands on his hips, looking utterly uncomfortable.

"What part of 'I need a minute' was confusing to you?"

His shirt was still MIA, and his abs flexed and chest lifted as he inhaled deeply. "Who is Adam?"

"None of your fucking business. Go away."

Jenner's throat moved as he swallowed hard, but he definitely didn't go away. Instead, he sat beside her, leaned up on her tree of shame and brought yet another round of heat flooding into her cheeks.

"I shouldn't have done that," he murmured. "I shouldn't have kissed you and lost control. I had this plan to keep it professional and I…" He gritted his teeth and broke a twig in half. "I messed up. I'm sorry."

"Yeah, well, I wasn't sorry until just now. I actually wanted to be with you," she gritted out bitterly. "I thought my stupid dry spell would finally be over, and I could just get this thing over and done. Then it wouldn't be this huge, terrifying thing to me anymore."

"Get what done? Losing your virginity? Lena, it should be special for your first time."

"Oh yeah? Was it super special for your first time, Jenner?"

"Yeah, it was."

His answer drew her up short, so she jerked her gaze to his to gauge his seriousness. He wasn't teasing her, though. At least not that she could tell.

"You look surprised. What, you think a guy can't have his first time be special?"

"I don't know about guys, but from the way you just tossed me away back there, I thought maybe you were a player."

"No, Lena, I'm not a player." His voice was tired, and he chucked half of the broken stick into the woods as if her snap judgment offended him. "I was twenty before I lost mine. I had a girl I loved and sex with her meant something."

"What happened?" she asked softly.

Jenner made a clicking sound behind his teeth and picked up another limb. He stripped the leaves off it one by one, then said, "She got pregnant."

"You didn't want the baby?"

"Oh, I wanted the baby. More than anything. It was this instant family, you know? But my woman didn't really know me, didn't know my secrets, and apparently she was keeping some of her own. I was over the moon, twenty, ready to be a dad because I was going to do this better than how my dad did with me and my brothers. Except when we went to get the ultrasound, they told us the baby was a girl."

Baffled, Lena shook her head. "And you didn't want a girl?"

Jenner clutched his fist around the snapped twig and slid his sad blue gaze to her. "I can't have girls. She wasn't mine."

That didn't make any sense. "How do you know you can't have girls?"

"Because in my lineage, there have been zero female offspring for thousands of years. And when I told my woman that, she admitted she had someone else. Someone who was no good, not like I was to her, and she wanted me raising the baby instead of the other guy."

"And you couldn't?" Her whisper came out airy and devastated.

Jenner shook his head. "Not after all the lies. I couldn't trust her. I haven't told anyone that ever. Not even my brothers, so now it's your turn. Who is Adam?"

"Adam was my best friend."

"I thought you said he was your husband."

"Isn't that the way love should be, though? Friends first? We lived next door to each other growing up. Walked to school together, did our homework together. He used to sneak into my house and sleep in my bed when his parents argued. Even when he got popular in high school, he never made me feel like I wasn't his world, you know? And it was never love, nothing like that. We were just...best friends. But when we were seniors in high school, he had this bruise on his leg that wouldn't heal. He went to the doctor and was diagnosed with leukemia. I went to every appointment, nearly flunked out and only graduated because some of my teachers had pity on me. I spent every day with him. Cut class when he wasn't strong enough to go to school anymore. And one day, when we were lying on his bed, he asked me to marry him. He was his parents' only son, and his mom had been crying over never watching him get married, so he asked me, and I said yes." Lena's bottom lip trembled too hard to go on, and a warm tear slid down her cheek. She swallowed, over and over, trying to regain her composure. "We were married three months before he passed. He was so sick..." She wiped the moisture from her cheek. "He wasn't up for consummating the marriage."

"Jesus," Jenner murmured as he draped his arm across her shoulders and pulled her tight against his side. "I'm so sorry." His hand cradled her cheek, so she pressed her palm against his knuckles to keep his touch there because she needed this. He hadn't told anyone about the woman who had broken his heart, and she understood that because Lena had never talked to anyone about Adam either. It had been too painful to relive.

"I didn't mean to be a twenty-six-year-old virgin, Jenner. God, I hate the way you looked at me when you found out. I just wasn't ready to be intimate with a man for a long time after Adam because it felt like a betrayal to his memory. And when I was finally ready, I was full-on running—travelling constantly and never staying in one place long enough to meet a nice guy I trusted enough to sleep with."

"And you trust me? Woman, I almost fucked you doggy style in the woods, directly following our first kiss. I'm not trustworthy with shit like this. I'm too rough, and I lose my mind—"

"And I understood that going into it, you ridiculous man. I wasn't looking for candles, fireworks, and opera music. Maybe I did at one time, but the longer I go without *it* happening, the more intimidated I feel. No, I didn't want a rough fucking from behind for my first time," she said through a thick laugh. "But somewhere in the middle would've been nice." Lena wiped her damp cheeks with the back of her hand and said, "And furthermore, I'm scandalous."

Jenner chuckled deep in his throat. "Oh, yeah?"

BEAR FUR HIRE | T. S. JOYCE

"I own a sex book with pictures, have let two boys finger me, and I watched a porn once. I'm practically a professional sexer without, you know, actually doing the deed."

Jenner was laughing now, head thrown back, bright white smile easy as the sound of his amusement ricocheted through the quiet woods.

"You're laughing, but it's true."

Jenner stood, then offered his hand to help her up. "I'm sure you will rock a man's world when the time comes."

Lena allowed him to pull her up, and she dusted the seat of her pants, smiling sadly. "That man isn't going to be you, is it?"

Jenner licked his lips, the smile fading from his face, and shook his head. "I'm not the right fit for you."

"Oh." She dropped her gaze to his boots so she wouldn't be tempted to stare at his eight pack abs as heat flushed her cheeks.

"Hey," he murmured, lifting her chin until she met his gaze. "It has nothing to do with whether I'm attracted to you or not. I'm just not gentle enough, you understand?"

"Of course." But she didn't. As he walked back toward the horses, pulling his shirt on as he went, she was more confused by him than ever. She'd practically offered herself on a silver platter, and he wasn't interested in even trying to be gentle with her?

Dalton had been right. Jenner wasn't the right man to give her heart.

Too bad she hadn't listened.

SIX

Dammit, that had been close. Too close. Jenner slung his leg over his horse's saddle and scrubbed his hand over his face to try and clear the visions that were running a loop across his mind. Her lips parted for him. The feel of her perfect, soft tit in his palm. His hand between her legs. So wet for him. The small, needy gasps she gave him every time he touched her skin. And the look of heart-stomping disappointment on her face when he'd scrambled away from her. Blame it on her dropping the V-bomb all he wanted to, but it was bullshit. That entire sexy encounter had been his fault. He'd kissed her angry, unable to help himself, gotten turned on as fuck when she'd slapped him, and then he'd taken everything way too far, way too fast.

He couldn't even look at Lena as she hoisted herself into the saddle. She smelled so good right now, like pheromones and sex, and it was all for him.

Six hours. He'd made it six hours before going after her. It wasn't because he'd been in a dry spell with women either. Lena called to his bear in ways that were terrifying. He was the one in control. Out of his brothers, Tobias and Ian, he had been the one with the most restraint, and now look at him. Around Lena, he always felt on the verge of a Change, and for no damned reason other than he was trying to deny his feelings for her. His inner bear didn't like that. *Mine.* The word brushed his mind every half an hour, at least. He wanted her so bad it was hard to look away from her, but just as hard to see her hurting because of him. Trapped. A couple of days, and she'd trapped him as surely as Brea had.

Jenner kicked his horse and cast Lena a quick glance to make sure she was following. She wouldn't meet his gaze, and it ripped him up. He'd done that—made her feel less than.

He'd bonded before. Age twenty, cocky as hell and ready to conquer the world, he'd met Brea right out of hibernation. And for that warm season, he'd been blindingly happy. Six months felt like forever, but it wasn't until later he realized it was his bear forging a bond that had nothing to do with compatibility and everything to do with instinct. To his knowledge, Ian and Tobias hadn't had those urges until

Ian went and got himself married last month. He'd gone to that wedding because Elyse had begged him to go, but that wasn't the only reason he'd made the trip to his brother's and new mate's homestead. Jenner had wanted to see for himself if what Ian and Elyse had was real because, dammit, after Brea, Jenner had been convinced the instinct to procreate and pair up trumped love matches. But Elyse had been as smitten with Ian as his brother had been with her, and the look in their eyes as they said their vows had dumped Jenner's world upside down. They weren't paired up because Ian's bear wanted cubs. On the contrary, Ian didn't want cubs at all. Didn't want his sons to face hibernation like the rest of their lineage. No, Ian had paired up with Elyse because he, as well as his bear, were completely and ridiculously devoted to the woman.

Jenner wanted that.

Now that there was hope for a loving match for a monster like him, it was impossible not to think about Lena as his mate. It was hard to hate the bond that he could feel forming between them. But she had a life and an important job that required her to travel all over the world. He couldn't strap her to Alaska and to six months of cold and loneliness every year when he went to sleep each winter. It wasn't fair to her.

Sex with her would make it impossible to let her go. Sex would seal their bond and sever any chance he had of moving on. The only reason he'd been able to break the bond with Brea was that his bear was a true animal and couldn't stand the thought of raising another man's child. If he was just a man, perhaps he could've looked past the fact that she'd started their relationship newly pregnant. Perhaps he could've even gotten over the lies and trusted her eventually. But he was only half man, and his animal side had revolted the moment that doctor told them she was having a girl—another male's offspring. Bear shifters, as well as wolf shifters, didn't produce female children.

And after Brea, he'd been jaded, convinced that love was reserved for good, normal people—not an animal like him.

But Lena…

Lena felt like everything. She felt like hope.

Jenner had been sleepwalking for so long, stuck in the dark, going through the motions. Sleep in the winter, eat and work during the summer, rinse and repeat forever. But she'd just come in and taken an ice pick to the permafrost he'd built up to protect his heart, and she was slamming that blade against him with shattering blows. When she looked at him like he was important, *crack*. When she'd bandaged him so fearlessly, *crack*. Every time she touched him, *crack*. When she'd wanted him out there by that pond, trusting him completely with her virginity, trusting him with something so important and fragile...*crack, crack, boom.*

But what the fuck could he offer her? She was successful, headstrong, independent, and leather-tough. He was outmatched. He was a hunting guide with a tendency to drop off the face of the planet from October to April every year, and she was a woman with her life figured out and an incredible future in front of her.

She was oil, and he was water, and they could never really work.

The kindest thing he could do for Lena was find her the brown bears, get her the pictures that would skyrocket her career, take her back to the lodge, and wave her off when Tobias flew her out of here and back to her life. The thought of her leaving socked him in the middle and made it hard to breathe, but she deserved better. Better than him and better than the life and heartache he would strap her with. Bear shifters were meant to be alone. Dad was proof, and Ian was the exception.

What happened at the pond with Lena couldn't ever happen again.

After losing her first mate the way she did, even if she and Adam had just been friends, she deserved for the next man she chose to stick.

Bear shifters were genetically prone to disappoint, and Lena was special.

No matter how much he'd come to care for her, Jenner wouldn't hold her back for his own selfish gains.

SEVEN

Jenner had barely strung a sentence together since their little make-out then freak-out session earlier. Lena was usually perfectly content to be quiet on trips like this. She'd had several guides, usually of the old, tough, burly mountain man variety that were respectful and professional with little to say. But she didn't want that with Jenner. She wanted more. Problem was, he definitely did not, and now she had been stuck behind him all day, unable to stop looking at him, unable to stop thinking about him, unable to stop wanting him to turn in his saddle and tell her everything would be okay and they would go back to the way they were before they laid everything bare in the woods earlier.

His distance made her physically ache.

The sun sat low in the sky, streaking the horizon with pinks and oranges, and suddenly, Jenner pulled his horse off toward a line of trees. There was an old, ash-filled fire pit dug into the ground and logs laid around it to sit on. Off to the side of the small clearing was an old corral made of gray, splintered wood and barbed wire.

Jenner walked his lead horse right through the open gate and dismounted. "We call this Wolf Camp."

"Wolf Camp? Why?"

"Dalton and Chance built it up when we first started scouting this way."

"Okay, what does that have to do with wolves?"

Jenner narrowed his eyes thoughtfully at her, then suddenly became very busy unpacking saddlebags.

"Okay then," she muttered, dismounting. "Fantastic conversation."

Gunner was apparently too tired to give her any shit as she unsaddled him, and when the beast was freed from his restraints, he headed to a long trough that was filled with recent rainwater. Jenner carried a ridiculously heavy amount of their supplies in his arms while she carried the pack of camera equipment.

Jenner didn't talk to her while they built the tent, and he didn't say a word when he disappeared toward the sound of running water with a bucket. He didn't even strike up a conversation while he built a fire or cooked butter-soaked potatoes in foil and skewers of beef and vegetables over the open flame. All the while, he did his best to ignore her completely. She waited to see that striking flash of blue in his eyes, but she never did.

Lena pulled on her jacket and settled in to sketch in her notebook while the fire crackled and sparked against the darkening night.

She thought she could feel his eyes on her now and again, but when she looked up, his attention was always on the flames.

"It's best this way," he muttered, elbows on his knees as he sat on one of the logs by the fire. And there was that blue, at last. "I wasn't professional before."

Pursing her lips, she nodded her head. "Professional."

"Yeah, professional. This is my job. It's what I love to do, and you should know I haven't ever done that with a woman I've taken out before. I lost my head."

"Me, too."

"I shouldn't have told you about Brea."

"Jenner! I get it, okay? Please don't sit here and talk about how you regret every conversation we've had. I haven't talked about Adam either, but for fuck's sake, I'm not taking it back. It felt good for a minute, sharing that part of myself with someone else. I understand. I really do. If you have to ignore me to get us back to a guide-client relationship, fine. But don't make me feel bad for having a vulnerable moment with you."

After a few awkward minutes, Jenner cleared his throat. "So, what have you photographed before?" The question was stiff and formal and made her want to curl her lip up in a snarl. It was a distancing question, but she was tired and sore from the saddle and wholly uninterested in back-peddling with the baffling man tonight.

Lena shook her head and went back to sketching. "Fuck off, Jenner."

"What are you sketching?"

Lena frowned down at the picture of Jenner's face. She was currently shading his eyes. They looked empty and distant, but his dark brows were drawn down as if he were lost in thought. "Wolves."

He gripped a metal mug in his hands and sighed. "I can hear a lie."

"Great for you," she snapped, slamming the sketchbook closed and shoving it into her satchel. "And you can growl and smell moose and tell when I'm on my period and turn off your warmth like a switch. Color me impressed. I'm going to wash up in the creek." She snatched her backpack and strode off into the trees toward the sound of gurgling water.

Behind her, the *clang* of a metal cup smashing against a tree echoed through the quiet forest. She tossed a glance over her shoulder, but Jenner was standing with his back to her, his hands linked behind his head, looking up at the sky. His shoulders looked tense and his silhouette rigid. If he was pissed, so what? She'd slowly burned in his silence all day. They'd shared a monumental moment earlier, and then he'd emotionally shoved her away. This sucked. It was an awful feeling right now, knowing the rest of the trip would be like this. Torture.

There was a thin trail that led to the dark sandbank of the river. Her boots squished across the damp earth until she reached the gently lapping waves. In the distance, thunder rolled and the clouds lit up with a flash of lightning. The storm was still far away, but she could smell the rain. Bottle of body wash and plastic cup in hand, she kicked out of her boots. From here, the creek looked like it was only knee-deep. A moment of modesty took her, and she twisted around to make sure Jenner wasn't there, just in case. But no, he wouldn't follow her out here. Not as uninterested as he was, so she was safe to undress. The water was cold against her ankles, and she gasped as she made her way to the deepest part. She bathed and washed her hair as fast as she was able, then tossed her toiletries up on the bank and sank down into the waves to rinse off. She got used to the water, little by little, and then the air became colder than the water. She lifted her face to the moon, sitting heavy and low and half hidden by the approaching storm clouds. Around her, the wind brushed the tall grass this way and that, and as she wrung water from her hair, she smiled up at Mother Moon, who was drawing long notes from distant wolves, howling at her beauty as the lightning lit up the distant clouds.

A limb snapped, and Lena jerked her gaze to the bank behind her.

Jenner sat on a grassy ledge as though he'd been there the entire time. The limb she'd heard breaking was between his fingers. Of course a wild thing like Jenner Silver wouldn't have been careless enough to let her hear his approach.

Chills blasted up her arms, and she clutched them over her chest, shielding her breasts even though she was sitting with her back to him.

When Jenner lifted that striking gaze to her, even brighter in the moonlight, he looked troubled. "You shouldn't be out here alone. This is brown bear country."

Lena huffed and returned her gaze to the moon. "I'm sure you would hear danger coming from a mile away."

"Even so."

"I'm not decent, Jenner. If you want to cling to our professional relationship, you should go back to camp."

There was a shuffling of fabric, but she'd be damned if she watched after him pathetically as he left.

When he brushed her shoulder, she stiffened, startled that he was still here at all. He sat in the waves behind her, legs encasing her on either side.

"What are you doing?" she asked on a shocked breath.

Jenner brushed her damp hair off her shoulder and kissed her neck. Pulling her back against his erection, he whispered, "This is a mistake."

She bristled at that word. "Jenner, I don't want to be anyone's mistake."

"No, woman. I mean, every part of me wants to be with you, and if we do this, I won't want you to leave."

She sighed a long exhalation and relaxed against him as he nibbled at the edge of her ear. She didn't want to talk about leaving. Not now. Not here with a man she was falling so breathlessly hard for. She'd never had such an instant connection with anyone in her life.

Jenner ran his fingertips lightly up her arms, dragging trails of fire with his touch. Moving her wet hair to the other side of her neck, he kissed her on the curve of sensitive skin that arched from her ear to the tip of her shoulder. His lips moved against her so gently she rolled her eyes closed, forsaking the beautiful moon and oncoming storm clouds to give herself completely to this moment. He took his time, kissing, nibbling, sucking, and every once in a while, he would bite her hard enough that her skin would tingle, and then he would be gentle again.

Jenner was worshipping her body, unrushed and unbidden. The rough man who had lost control earlier and had come close to taking her from behind didn't exist here. Not tonight.

Gentle kisses, nibble, teeth. His hand cupped the other side of her neck as he grazed his teeth harder against her skin. His erection was thick and hard against her back, and he rolled his hips gently with the next nibble. "Lena," he whispered. "You should tell me not to bite you."

Confused, she frowned up at the moon and angled her head to give him better access to her skin as he sucked. "But it feels good when you bite me."

"Not like this. Tell me, or I'll stop here. Order me, Lena. Do it now."

"Don't bite me, Jenner."

A soft rumble rattled his chest and vibrated against her back, but before she could ask about it, he was up with her folded in his arms, dragging his legs with powerful strides through the shallow waves toward the beach.

She was shocked with this surreal moment. Water drops zigzagged down his scarred torso, and she traced one with her fingertip. They were both cast in blue hues thanks to the moonlight, and every time lightning struck, it illuminated the long silver marks on his body. He looked fierce, like a warrior. Lethal and beautiful. Hers. She kissed a pair of marks over his heart and smiled when she felt his heart pounding against her lips.

Jenner jerked to a stop, and when she lifted her gaze to his, he looked lightning struck himself. "What was that for?" he asked so softly she almost didn't hear his words over the wind.

"I like the way you look."

He settled her on her feet and looked down at his chest, then back to her, his eyes tight with uncertainty. "How can you? I look…" Jenner ripped his gaze away from her, but not before she saw the disgust there.

Slowly, she slid her arms around his neck. "You look perfect to me. Someday you're going to tell me what happened to you, and I'll like your scars even more."

He gripped her arms as if he was thinking about pulling her touch off him. "You won't."

Lena stood up on tiptoes and kissed him softly, just a brush of her lips to tell him she was in this. "You don't know me yet, but you will. You don't trust me yet…" She cupped his cheeks and dragged his gaze to hers. "But you *will*. I've never seen a man more suited to me, Jenner Silver." She smiled absently and kissed a long mark that ran the length of his collarbone. "Jenner Silver, bearer of silver scars. Who have you shared these with?"

His Adam's apple bobbed as he shook his head slow, drawing a satisfied smile from her lips.

"Good." She traced the latticework of the old marks. "This treasure map is only for me."

Jenner shivered under her touch and rolled his eyes closed for a second, and when he opened them again, they looked darker somehow.

"I'll be gentle with you," he promised. His voice was gravelly, tapering into a low humming that barely registered. "You deserve gentle."

"Okay," she murmured. Maybe it was hard for men to be gentle. Or perhaps it was just big, dominant brawlers like Jenner who had trouble taking it slow with a woman. She didn't have enough experience to understand why his declaration sounded so much like an oath.

Jenner cupped the back of her neck and lowered his lips against hers. The second their skin touched, a drum of thunder rolled in the distance, so loud it vibrated through her chest. Or perhaps the deep sound had rattled from Jenner. He angled his head and deepened their kiss, pushing his tongue gently past her lips.

He eased her back, laid her down, but where she expected the shock of cold sand against her back, it was soft and warm instead. A blanket. He'd brought a blanket. He'd planned this and prepared for her comfort. Wild Jenner had compromised. He would bed her out in the wilderness where he was most at home, but he would make her comfortable.

And suddenly, she was devastatingly relieved she'd saved her first time for this moment. She would never forget this. His soft lips, his searching hands, cupping her breasts, brushing her ribcage, running down the length of her bent leg as he settled in the cradle she created between her knees. Lightning lit up the sky behind him, casting him in this otherworldly glow as his eyes looked volcanic and dark, hungry for her whenever he eased from her lips to look at her. This wasn't the passionate loss of self-control that they'd fallen into earlier. This was a conscious decision to let this be special. To allow them to bond in ways that would tether her heart to this masculine, capable, incredible man.

Right now, she couldn't help but feel utterly overwhelmed with how important he was. With a slight smile lifting one corner of his sensual lips, Jenner lowered his mouth to her breast and drew her nipple between his teeth. He sucked hard, and she gasped as her hips rolled against his in reaction. Oh, he could control her body. Could draw her emotions like he had direct access to her soul.

Lifting up, he hovered over her, stony torso in shadow, and long, thick shaft jutting between them, intimidating her completely.

"Jenner," she whispered, about to voice her concerns on the physics of their pairing, but he was busy working biting kisses down her belly and *oh!* Those sexy teeth of his grazed her inner thigh right before he kissed her sex, right where she was most sensitive. His body moved like water, rolling toward her with every thrust of his tongue, as if it was hard for him not to be touching her.

She couldn't believe this was happening. This big, beautiful, powerful man had his mouth on her sex, and from the hum that vibrated against her, he was enjoying himself. He thrusted harder into her then pulled away, and now his eyes were on fire. Fevered and hungry in the instant before he lowered his body onto hers and pressed the head of his cock against her sex. Lena clutched his shoulders just to anchor herself. She felt like she was floating or falling, and her stomach dipped dangerously as his lips brushed her neck again.

"I won't bite you," he murmured, but it sounded like he was trying to convince himself more than her.

She rolled her hips, and he jerked in response, breath ragged. His fingers gripped the back of her hair gently as he pushed into her slowly, inch by inch. She was tight, and it burned, but he was taking her body in such a way that the pleasure of being connected with him outweighed any pain. His second slow thrust hurt less as her body adjusted to his size, and she ran her fingertips down the curve of his stony arms, flexed and trembling slightly, as if he was holding himself back. Someday she would beg him to be himself—to ruck her up, but not tonight. Tonight, he'd been right. She did need gentle. She needed this—soft sighs, moonlight, control, his eyes on her, that bewildered, intense look on his face that said he was falling as hard as she was. His slow pace stole her nerves away and allowed her to get lost in this moment with him. The next time he rocked into her, she moved with him, gaining confidence with the languid pace he set.

He stretched her, filled her, built the tingling pressure in her middle, then gave her relief every time he slid out. How could anything feel this good? How had she gone her entire life without knowing this kind of connection with a man? That answer was easy. Because she hadn't met Jenner yet. Jenner was meant to give her this moment, and all the waiting had been worth it.

He let off a sexy moan that said his control was slipping, and when she whispered his name, he closed his eyes tight and bucked into her faster.

"Lena," he rasped as his teeth hit her shoulder. His hands tightened in her hair, and she was so close, toeing the edge, about to spill over.

And as he slid into her again and again, she knew she was done for. This felt too big. Too essential. Jenner was doing something to her body, binding her to him. She was changing from her marrow outward, and for a moment, it was terrifying, exciting, overwhelming, and perfect.

With a soft gasp, she looked up at him, and he had her. His gaze was so open. So vulnerable. So caring. He was swelling inside of her with each thrust now, pumping faster. Eyes closed and robbing her of that strange, changing color, he rested his forehead against hers and gritted his teeth as a long snarl rattled his chest.

It was that noise that did it. Bowing back against the blanket, she closed her eyes as she detonated around him, pulsing hard, each burst of pleasure feeling better than the last.

Jenner slammed into her now, over and over, faster until he froze and gripped her against him. Warmth spilled into her in hot jets, heating her from the inside out. And as he emptied himself, Jenner did something that baffled her completely. He slowed his pace and began to build the pressure in her middle a second time. But this time around, he kissed her gently until she came again, one orgasm rolling into the next. He hadn't just flopped over and enjoyed being sated. He'd given her even more of himself and taken care of her needs completely.

She didn't mean for the tears that rimmed her eyes as she melted into his gentle kiss. She'd never been a woman who cried much, but he'd just touched her heart in ways she hadn't thought possible.

Jenner eased back, still buried deep within her and apparently content to feel every aftershock from her. "Hey," he murmured, his face transforming into a worried frown. He smoothed her hair back with a gentle touch. Running the pad of his thumb across her temple, he frowned, then looked at the drop of moisture there with such confusion. "Did I hurt you?"

Lena's face crumpled as another tear streamed out of the corner of her eye. She shook her head and pulled his palm to her lips. A long kiss on his hand allowed her to stall so that her voice wouldn't come out fragile and small. "I'm happy."

Jenner let off a sigh, and his eyes softened immediately over the smile that transformed his face. "Good. That was…" He shrugged his shoulders and looked completely lost for words, but she understood.

"For me, too."

His lips lifted in a bigger smile just as he lowered them to hers. His kiss made her want to cry harder, which was ridiculous. Why did she feel so raw and open right now? This wasn't what she'd imagined it would be like. It was as if Jenner was welding her broken pieces back together.

She clung to his shoulders as he eased out of her, then he rocked them upward. Hand on the creases behind her knees, Jenner pulled her legs around him, stood, then walked them slowly into the creek and lowered them into the waves. With a gentle touch, he cleaned her in the water. She was in so deep with him now. The well of her emotion was bottomless as he kissed her with sweet, biting pecks.

With a grin, she bit him back, pulling on his lip for a moment before she released him. Hugging him close and resting her chin on his shoulder, she murmured against his ear, "My wild Jenner."

The soft growl rattled his throat again, and her grin widened. He'd spent so much time with the animals, he'd become one somewhere along the way. And for some reason, that fact made her love him even more. Love? Her heart stuttered, and she hugged him tighter so he wouldn't see the confusion on her face. Burying her face against his neck, she sighed, unsure of whether to be terrified of the emotion or to be happy she was capable of feeling love for a man at all. Through the years, she'd been afraid that part of her heart had been too damaged.

Lightning flashed closer, followed immediately by loud, rumbling thunder, and the clouds opened up, dumping hard rain down on them, splatting in a stinging cadence onto her bare skin.

Jenner's laugh was infectious and drew giggles from her as he stood them up. Pulling her hand, he led her toward their clothes where they gathered the blanket and belongings, shoved their feet into their hiking boots, and bolted through the pouring rain toward camp.

And he gave her another gift, another moment—one she would remember for always.

Right as they made it into the circle of lantern light near the tent, he turned and graced her with a smile that stopped her heart. It was devastatingly happy and open. His body was built like a brick house and sexy as hell, but that smile showed the man underneath it all. And he was giving that smile to her. *Her.* His eyes were vivid blue and dancing, the angles of his face sharp as glass, and right here, in this moment, she got her first glimpse of two shallow dimples that bracketed his mouth. His dark hair was soaked, and tiny drops of water clung to the ends, ready to fall, and when she stumbled, he picked her up like she weighed nothing, hustled her into the tent, and then disappeared back out of the flap.

Shocked at how utterly changed she felt, she stood there naked, dripping into her untied hiking boots, arms full of her belongings. She watched Jenner as he pulled a covered Dutch oven from beside the fire and snatched the lantern.

His wide shoulders blocked out the rain completely as he ducked through the tent opening, and after he'd zipped them safely inside, he turned that grin on her again. "You hungry?"

Was she ever. His abs were flexing with every breath, his body tight like a bowstring, and she'd just been with him. Hungry for food and hungry for Jenner, she nodded.

"Good."

"Good?"

"Yeah," he said, the smile slipping from his face. "I want to take care of you tonight. I want to feed you." His words had gone low and gravelly again, and a delicious shiver zipped up her spine.

"I'd like that." Did she need a man to take care of her? No, but with Jenner things were different. She didn't mind being vulnerable with him.

She had one towel in her bag and dried off as best as she could before she got into her comfortable night clothes. Her hair was going to dry wild, but from the way Jenner kept slipping her hungry glances, she didn't think he would mind au naturale. Which made sense. Only a wild woman would do for a feral man like him.

He slid into a pair of jeans but left his shirt off, thank heavens for tiny blessings. His pants were low enough that she still had a fantastic view of those sexy strips of muscle that wrapped around his hips. And as she spread out a sleeping bag to the sound of the pattering rain against the tent, Jenner loaded up two metal plates with steak, vegetables, and steaming baked potatoes. It all smelled so good, her stomach growled, so she wrapped her arms around her middle with a giggle.

He set up their dinner on the sleeping bag picnic style and sat directly across from her. It wasn't until midway through the meal that he stopped with a knowing grin and asked, "Was it everything you imagined it would be?"

"No." Heat flooded her cheeks, so she ducked her gaze to her plate of food. "It was much more."

Jenner hooked a hand under her chin and pulled her face up to meet his. With a light kiss, he settled back in front of his plate and murmured, "I hate when you hide your blushes from me. I've never met a woman who colors up so pretty." He swallowed hard, his eyes growing serious. "I've never met a woman so pretty."

"You're teasing. I bet you say that to every girl you take to bed."

His dark eyebrows arched high, and he let out a surprised laugh. "Is that what you think of me?"

"Well…yeah. Look at you."

And he did. He ran a quick glance over his bare torso and gave her an uncertain half smile as if he thought she was the one teasing now. "Yeah, I'm a great catch. Scarred up hunting guide, off in the woods most of the time, prefers to be alone, emotionally constipated, and sleeps half the damned—" Jenner dropped his gaze and cleared his throat, attention back on his food.

"Day away? I like naps, too. That won't scare me off."

But the smile she'd been trying to conjure didn't return.

"I have six sisters," she said low, desperate not to let their connection go just yet.

"Six?"

"Yep. It was an all girls' club growing up, especially after Dad passed. He wanted a son so badly that he and my mom just kept trying."

"Let me guess. You're the oldest."

"What makes you think that?"

"Super responsible, looking out for others, independent."

"Wrong, wrong, dead wrong. I'm the baby of the family. And"—she scrunched up her nose in disbelief she was about to admit this out loud—"the black sheep of the Rhodes family."

"No."

She laughed and tossed a pepper at him. "It's true. My sisters are all married or engaged. Three of them have given my mom grandbabies, and all of them were settled by my age. Every time I go back for the holidays, I get so excited about seeing everyone and connecting again, and then after about a day with them, I'm clawing my eyeballs out to leave again."

"Why?"

Lena sighed and lifted her shoulders to her ears in a shrug. "I don't know."

"Yes, you do. Why do you run?"

She bit her bottom lip and pushed a piece of steak around her plate. "Because that was supposed to be me."

"You and Adam?"

She nodded and huffed a laugh. "Sounds so stupid because it was a marriage out of friendship, but I was eighteen and hoping and praying on my knees every night that Adam would pull through, and then I was widowed three weeks after I turned nineteen. I was so young, you know? And for a minute, my life had made sense, and then all the sudden it didn't anymore, and I didn't know how to stop the tailspin. Every time I go back home, I have to hear the speeches about how it's time I moved on, and I get so angry at them. It's so easy for people to say that. Easy to say and almost impossible to do. It's so flippant. Just, 'Lena, you need a man.' But I had one, and I didn't recover. Every time I go home, I come out of it eager to travel again for this job. I take more assignments than anyone else because I have no one tying me to anything."

Jenner's eyes were on her, sad but understanding.

"I guess I'm still in the tailspin, huh?"

"My brother was the one that made these," he murmured, gesturing to the long silver slashes across his chest. "I understand tailspins."

Shocked, Lena stared in horror at his scarred up torso. "Your brother did that how?"

Jenner shook his head. "He didn't mean to. My other brother Ian saved me, but barely."

"You have two brothers?"

A smile stuttered across his face. "We're triplets. Multiples are common in my lineage."

"You're a triplet?" Her voice had jacked up an octave. "I don't even think I've met a twin before. Can you read each other's minds?"

He laughed. "No. I've only seen them a handful of times in the last few years, and most of that has been recently."

"Why?"

"We don't get along so well. We try, but there is just a part of us that is too competitive to spend any actual quality time together. One of my brother's, Ian, he regrets the broken relationship. He's always tried to reach out, and I've swatted him down. Tobias is even worse than I am."

"Wait, so which brother did that?" she asked, flicking her fingers toward his silver scars.

"Tobias."

"What? I flew in a plane with him! Is he dangerous?"

"Yes, but not to you. And this was an accident. It happened when we were sixteen."

"You said Ian saved you. Where were your parents?"

"Uh." He sat up straighter and wiped his hands, clearly uncomfortable with where the discussion had ended up. "Mom wasn't in the picture. She couldn't handle multiples, and Dad was more of a hands-off kind of parent. He wanted us to figure everything out on our own. Ian, Tobias, and I were kicked out of the nest at sixteen, and the accident happened right after that."

"Oh, Jenner. Do you think that is part of the reason for the rift? Maybe Tobias feels badly."

"Tobias doesn't feel anything."

The food sat in a lump in her stomach, so she pushed the plate away and drew her knees up to her chest to ward off the chill that was suddenly rippling gooseflesh over her arms. "I'm sorry."

He watched her quietly, head canted as if he couldn't figure her out. "You're different from other people. Different to me. You don't mind things about me that make others uncomfortable."

"Like what?"

"Like that heaviness in the air that has you drawing into yourself. That's me. Most people move away from it on instinct, but not you. When the air around me gets heavy, you stop ducking your gaze and look right into my eyes. You're doing it now."

"I told you I was broken," she whispered, frozen in his predator gaze.

"Mmm," he rumbled. "You are the least broken person I've ever met."

She bit her trembling bottom lip to steady her emotions. "That's one of the nicest things anyone has ever said to me."

He huffed a breath and stood, taking their plates with him. He'd finished off four baked potatoes and a mound of other food while she'd only been able to finish two-thirds of her plate. Confused by his abrupt escape, she readied for bed, then pulled on her jacket and stepped outside to brush her teeth. The rain had slowed to a drizzle, but she still pulled her hood over her head.

Jenner was leaned against a tree near the corral, as still as a sentry in the soft glow of a lantern he'd hung from a low branch beside him. Only his eyes moved as he followed her path toward a canteen that sat on a splintered table.

Teeth brushed and mouth rinsed, she turned for the tent, but stopped before she went inside. "Jenner?"

"Yeah?"

"Did I say something wrong?"

"You've done nothing wrong, woman."

"Are you going to stay out here all night?"

"I have to keep you safe."

"But—"

"You don't understand, Lena. I have to."

"You always sleep in the rough to protect clients?" He was making no sense. It was raining and chilly, and he could get sick staying out all night in this weather when they had a perfectly dry tent right here.

"You're more than a client now," he said quietly, his eyes troubled.

"Okay." She shifted her weight side to side, stalling. After what they'd done by the creek, she didn't want to say goodnight right now. "Jenner, can you just lay by me for a little while then?"

The steely look in his eyes softened, and he nodded his chin once. "Just until you fall asleep."

A small victory, but a victory all the same. She hid her triumphant smile as he followed her inside. He lay down and held his arm out for her to cuddle against his side, and damn her emotions, the gesture almost made her want to cry again. Jenner was hard. Iron-tough and cold to others. She'd seen it when they'd been at the lodge. He could joke with the other guides, but from a distance. With her, he was letting her in little by little. He was exposing his softer side to her, and if that didn't prove he was growing to trust her, she didn't know what did.

She rested her cheek against his warm chest and traced the crisscrossing scars across his ribs. Quietly, so as not to spoil the magic of this intimacy, she said, "You said I would like you less when I found out the reason behind these, but I like you more." *I love you, actually.* She left those words unspoken, though, because she hadn't said them to a man before, and Jenner seemed the type to run from something that serious this soon. She would be patient and hope that his feelings caught up with hers someday.

His heartbeat was steady and strong under her cheek, and his lips pressed against the top of her hair, lingering there while he pulled another unzipped sleeping bag over them. He turned off the lantern, and the soft rain pitter pattered against the nylon of the tent.

In the dark, Lena curled against him and let the warmth Jenner provided slip over her. She fought to keep her eyes open for a little while longer because this was another moment. Another gift added to the many he'd given her today.

"Jenner," she said sleepily.

"Hmm?" he rumbled in that sexy, deep timbre of his.

"I'm glad you were my first."

And as she drifted off, warm and safe against him, she could've sworn he whispered, "So am I."

EIGHT

Jenner resisted the urge to look back at Lena for the billionth time since they'd left Wolf Camp this morning. The deeper they got into brown bear country, the more he had to fight the instinct to turn around and take her back to the lodge where she would be safe. Because out here in this brutal wilderness, he wasn't the only monster anymore.

Behind him, Lena was clicking away on her camera, and for as wary as he was of taking his mate deep into bear country, he looked around and tried to see what she saw.

This land had always called to him, but she'd shown him a couple of pictures she'd taken this morning while he'd been packing up camp, and he'd been stunned into silence as he'd cradled the camera and looked at the images she'd captured. The splintered railing of the corral had been at the forefront in one of the photographs, and behind it, the packhorses were resting with their noses beside each other.

She'd discovered this moment of incredible serenity while he'd been rushing around trying to prepare for the rest of their trip. Lena saw the world differently. She found moments that he would've just walked by and never noticed. He didn't have a creative bone in his body, but Lena had the uncanny ability to find beauty in the mundane. The proof of that was the way she looked at his body, as if he was some priceless artwork instead of a slashed-up man.

The smell of fur brushed his oversensitive nose, and he inhaled deeply, jerking his attention to the woods where it came from. They were close now, in the thick of the brown bears. A couple of miles more, and they would be to the river.

An overwhelming need to protect Lena washed over him again. His instincts had kicked up the second he'd decided to have sex with her. He'd been mistaken that it took the act of sex to bind them because just the conscious decision to sleep with her made his bear draw up and snarl his possessiveness. *Mine, mine, mine.* The smell of grizzly fur grew more pungent on the wind. Unable to keep his distance any longer, Jenner pulled his horse around at a trot, circling back until he was next to Lena's mount.

Her smile was bright and instant, settling his territorial bear with nothing more than a look. "Hey you." She lifted the camera under her chin and clicked a picture.

Jenner narrowed his eyes, but she looked so damned happy as she laughed, he couldn't bring himself to reprimand her this time. "I'm going to pull out my own camera and give you a taste of your own medicine if you aren't careful."

"You have a camera?"

"Lennard makes us all take one out in case we can get pictures for the website." He opened the flap of one of his saddle bags and dug to the bottom, then pulled out a small, black digital camera. Jenner turned it on and clicked her picture, only Lena didn't shy away from the camera like him. Instead, she posed all cute in the saddle and gave him one of those boner-inducing smiles she'd been gifting him all morning. And in that instant, he knew he wouldn't be showing Lennard any of the pictures from this trip. He chuckled and leaned over his saddle, guiding his horse closer. Cupping her cheek, he kissed her, brushing his tongue against hers once before the gait of their horses became disjointed and pulled them away from each other.

Lena clicked another picture of him.

Out of curiosity, he asked, "Why do you do that?"

"I do it when I like the way your face looks. You are a quiet man, a reserved man, and you have this ability to hold your face frozen when you don't want people seeing what you are thinking. But I can tell. It's in your eyes. I like the way you look right after you kiss me."

Dangerous, observant woman. Lena would guess what he was long before he was ready to tell her. The idea of her looking at him in disgust made his bear want to claw out of his skin, so Jenner cleared his throat and blinked hard to stifle the stabbing pain in his middle.

"Are you okay?" Lena asked, worry tainting her words.

"I'm fine. Listen, about the bears. We're close to the river, which means we have to be wary out here. We won't be talking as much, and no playing around until I have us somewhere safer to camp tonight, okay?"

Her pretty honey-brown eyes had gone round and serious, and for the first time since he'd met her, she gave off the faint smell of fear. "Okay."

"Lena, I won't let anything happen to you, do you hear me? There is no need to be scared. I'm here." Always.

She nodded, pursing her lips, and he wanted to kiss them soft again. Wanted to make her feel safe again, but she should be nervous. She needed to keep her wits about her and be wary about their surroundings as much as he was.

"When we're out there, the bears will likely be so engrossed with the salmon run, they won't pester us, but some get curious. It depends on the cast of bears in this territory. If they get too close, you do exactly what I say."

"Will you know some of the bears?"

He drew up straight in the saddle as if he'd been electrocuted. Had she already guessed what he was? "What?"

"Have you seen these bears before when you've been scouting?"

"Oh." His shoulders relaxed, and he huffed a relieved breath. "Yeah, I'll likely know most of them. But I'm serious, Lena. These aren't like black bears. If I tell you to do something, it's not up for discussion. You just do it, okay?"

"I will." She swallowed audibly. "I trust you."

Jenner had stared at her lips as she'd said those three words. *I trust you.* Her instincts really were broken then, but he couldn't get himself to tell her how wrong she was to give her trust to an animal like him. Selfishly, he wanted to revel in this moment because it was the first time anyone in his life had said that to him.

"You want to take me in those woods and do dirty things to me, don't you?" she asked, her soft brown eyes sparking with challenge.

"Woman, believe me when I say you don't want me covering you right now. You'll be sore from last night, and I won't be easy today. Don't tempt me, minx." Jenner kicked his horse and pulled in front of Gunner again.

Oh, he wanted her bad. Couldn't think about much else other than pinning her against a tree and claiming her completely. He wanted her from behind, a fresh bite mark from his teeth on her shoulder. If she knew about his dark needs, she wouldn't be teasing him.

Right now, he needed to focus on something other than claiming her body, though, and that was keeping her safe. Lena had become precious to him. Last night he'd slept the entire night with her, even though he'd only meant to let her fall asleep next to him. That shit couldn't happen again. She was clouding his judgement. He should've been out in the open, listening for danger all night, not letting the rain against the tent muddle his senses.

Did he want to take her in the woods and make her scream his name? Hell yeah, now more than ever. She was his. His Lena, his mate, and that faint scent of brown bear had him feeling desperate for the first time in his life. His insides were churning with something he didn't quite understand, and as he looked back at her, something slowly clicked into place.

For the first time ever, he was afraid.

He was afraid that he wouldn't be enough to keep her safe out here.

Ripping his gaze away from the fear in her eyes, fury flooded his veins. His inner monster pulsed within him, angry at this moment of weakness. He was beast, and none of these grizzlies out here had anything on him. With his life, he would protect Lena.

Fuck being afraid. He would keep her safe.

He had to.

She was his mate to protect now.

NINE

Lena had never felt as exposed as she did now, hiking beside Jenner through an open field. There was a grizzly eating vegetation to their left, but it was too far away to get a proper picture. And besides, that one didn't seem to be the one Jenner was hunting.

He gave the bear a slit-eyed glance, then inhaled deeply and led them toward the river, adjusting the strap of his rifle as he walked with long, deliberate strides beside her.

If Jenner was nervous, she couldn't tell. She, on the other hand, was shaking so badly that it was hard to walk in a straight line.

"You smell like fear, Lena. Cut that shit out. I've got you."

Like she could control it. Lena sniffed her shoulder but didn't smell anything other than the natural, eco-friendly body wash she'd used in the creek last night. She smelled like earth and pine sap, not terror. With a frown at Jenner, she wondered just how long he'd spent out in nature to take on such animalistic senses. She spent most of her time out of doors, and she didn't have the knack for finding animals based on a heightened sense of smell. He barely even looked for scat on the ground when he was tracking like she'd seen other guides do.

A large chocolate-colored bear climbed over the ridge of the river bank directly in front of them, less than a hundred yards away, and Lena jerked to a stop, heart pounding in her chest and breath frozen in her lungs. When it saw them, it hunched down, startled, then sauntered slowly toward them, eyes suspicious, ears alert. *Bucks and Backwoods* had sent her to grizzly behavior class, but all her training went right out the window when she saw how big they were in real life. The bear's bottom lip was relaxed, giving her the perfect view of the long canines, and with every step toward them, it gave a glimpse of six-inch black claws.

"Take your pictures, woman," Jenner murmured. To the bear, he said in a loud, confident voice, "Go around. No, go around!" He gestured smoothly to the bear, and for some reason, the animal actually altered its course.

Lena lifted her camera carefully and began to shoot the animal, one click after the other, sure that at any moment, it would charge and they would both be made into bear poop.

Slowly, eyes ever on them, the animal made its way in a long arch around, then disappeared into the woods they'd come from.

"Holy shit," she said on a breath. She reviewed the last couple of pictures and looked up in shock at Jenner. "I got him."

"Yeah, well, that *him* was a *her*, and she was a young bear, easily manipulated." Jenner grabbed Lena's hand and pulled her forward toward the river. "That was just the beginning."

As he led her to the edge of a small, grassy ledge that snaked parallel to the river bank, Lena's mouth dropped open and her eyes went so wide they ached. Jenner had been right about that bear being young. Lena had thought it massive, but it was a miniature compared to the five bruins in front of them, standing on a short waterfall and fishing in the river, waiting for salmon to jump.

And now even she could smell her fear.

Jenner's hand, big and strong, gripped the back of her neck, and his lips pressed onto hers. She froze, shocked, then leaned forward and kissed him back. Jenner eased off and rested his forehead against hers. "Lena, you have to keep calm or I won't be able to… You're making me feel like I need to defend you, and it's dangerous to be around them in that kind of mind-set. Keep your cool, breathe. I won't let anything happen to you. I promise." He straightened up and let off a sharp sigh, but his eyes looked strange. They were darker, and now she remembered how they'd changed color last night, too. They looked browner than blue, and this time, she couldn't blame it on a lightning storm behind him.

"Your eyes," she said on a breath, reaching for his cheek to touch just under the morphing color.

Jenner's dark eyebrow quirked up, and he grabbed her wrist so fast, he blurred. Canting his head and offering her a warning glance, he murmured low, "Not now. Take your pictures so I can get you back to camp." *In one piece.*

She narrowed her eyes as he gave her his back and crouched down, scanning the river and beyond. Until camp then, but they would definitely talk about his mood-ring eyes later.

At least Jenner had been a beautiful distraction. As she set up her tripod a few feet from the grassy ledge, some of her fear dissipated. And as the bears seemed to notice their presence one by one and immediately returned their interest back to fishing rather than chomping on her bones, Lena's anxiety evaporated even more.

Or maybe she was in shock. This all felt surreal as she clicked her camera into place on the tripod and adjusted the shutter speed to compensate for the clouds that had drifted back over the sun. Cloudy days were her favorite because it was like having the magic hours all day.

Exhaling a shaky breath, she began taking pictures of the river bears. And as the afternoon wore on, and the hours ticked by, she relaxed into a false sense of safety as she saw the world through the lens. It was an excellent coping mechanism since it distanced her from the monster grizzlies that were so close. A few long, charging strides and they could be on her, but here, looking through the lens of her camera, Lena could pretend she was at the zoo, taking pictures of caged animals like when she was a kid. Only here, Jenner was the cage.

After taking a shot of one of the brown bears standing atop the shallow waterfall catching a jumping salmon in mid-air, she grinned at Jenner and showed it to him.

"Money shot," she whispered. The bear was massive with a muscular hump between its mature shoulders, frozen on her camera, water drops streaming from the tail of the fish as it sailed through the air and straight toward the grizzly's open jaws.

Jenner scrolled through a couple more, a vacant smile on his lips until suddenly he jerked to a stop and lifted his gaze back to the river. "Shit," he muttered. "Let's go."

"What's wrong?"

"Titus is king here, and I'm not up for a brawl with him," Jenner said low as he shouldered her backpack.

Lena looked across to the other side of a river where an enormous brown bear was lumbering toward the fishing grounds, head low. The two bears nearest him, both puny in size comparatively, scattered when they saw him. As he approached the bank, it became clear he was a fighter because his face was scarred and one of his ears was missing. His neck was nearly bald of fur from all the scars in that area. Shit indeed.

Heart hammering, Lena picked up her tripod and backed away slowly. Jenner's hand was on the back of her neck, pushing her low as they moved away. Now, some of the bears Titus had intimidated off the river were headed their way, and Jenner muttered another curse as he pulled the rifle off his shoulder and slid a bullet into the chamber with the distinct crack of metal on metal. "Don't stop moving. Slow and steady and don't give any of them your back."

"Okay, but Jenner, they're coming this way." She held her camera steady at her chest and took picture after picture of the two bears running toward them, their eyes unfocused as they glanced back behind them at Titus.

"I see them."

"Jenner, they're still coming. I don't think they see us."

"Heyayay," Jenner said low.

Both bears swung their gaze directly at them before startling toward the left.

"Good bears. You see us? We're not here to hurt you." One curved toward them, ears flat, but Jenner called, "No no no no." His gun was up now as Lena continued backing toward the woods. He let off a low rumbling growl in his chest, and the bear veered away, eyeing them warily as it galloped for the woods behind the other one.

It all made sense now, that growl Jenner could make— the one that sounded so real—the one that could turn her on one moment and electrify the fine hairs on her body the next. He'd learned that out here. He'd practiced it so he could talk to the bears. Jenner Silver had learned how to fit into the dominance hierarchy with some of the most fearsome apex predators in existence. No wonder he was such a sought-after guide, and no wonder he had such a high success rate.

132

Jenner was as close to a grizzly as a human could make himself.

As she passed through the tree line, Jenner's hand clutching her jacket to keep her from tripping, a dark figure climbed up the river ledge. Lena gripped Jenner's arm and jerked her chin toward the river. Jenner had been searching the woods for the runaway bears, but at her gesture, he slid his gaze to where Titus was climbing up onto the grassy flatland.

"Go," Jenner whispered, pushing her behind a thick grove of evergreen trees.

She whimpered as the titan began to make his way in their direction. Jenner clapped his hand over her mouth and froze behind the tree cover. She couldn't watch Titus stalking them, so Lena focused instead on the muscle in Jenner's sharp jaw that twitched as he clenched his teeth. His eyes were fierce, intense on whatever Titus was doing, and there was no mistaking the color now. Dark brown, even darker than hers, and it wasn't just his pupils dilated either. The black middles were pinpoints as his gaze arched slowly with Titus's movement.

"Come on," he said on a breath, pulling her backward and to the right. "He's confused between our scent and the other bears. We have to go now. Fast but steady, okay?"

Jenner removed his hand from her mouth, but she couldn't speak now if she wanted to, so she nodded.

Behind them, a bear roared so loud the birds flew from the canopy above them. The hairs rose on the back of Lena's neck as she bolted in the direction they'd tied the horses.

.   The next two miles were brutal. With every step she grew more and more exhausted, and behind her, Jenner kept up constant whispered encouragement for her to keep going. The backs of her heels were blistered in her hiking boots by the time she heard the snort of one of the horses, and her limbs tingled like they'd fallen asleep. She blamed that on the adrenaline dump into her bloodstream. Any moment now, she knew Titus was going to appear beside them or she would hear his terrifying roar again.

Without a word, Jenner helped her into Gunner's saddle, packed her horse with the supplies they'd brought, then untied them all. He swung up onto his own horse and nudged him into a trot through the piney woods. And unlike their ride here earlier, Jenner didn't ignore her and trust her to follow. He looked back every few seconds, as if he couldn't keep his eyes off her when danger was this near.

The farther away they traveled, the more her racing heartbeat settled. They were okay, and she'd gotten a batch of incredible pictures today. Even if this was all she got to take, it was plenty to complete her assignment. Relief flooded her, and finally, she could draw a deep breath into her lungs again.

It was nearly dark when Jenner pulled off beside a pair of trees. He hadn't said a word since they'd left, and he didn't seem inclined to talk now as he pulled a rope from a tie on his saddle and strung it between the trees. His movements were smooth, lithe like an animal's, and he wouldn't meet her gaze.

Lena dismounted and tied off her horses.

"Jenner?"

He had his back angled to her as he unpacked the saddle bags, but at his name, his shoulders went rigid. Had she done something wrong? Maybe she hadn't run fast enough when he needed her to.

Steadying her trembling hands, she slid her palms up his back. "What's wrong?"

Jenner spun and dipped his mouth to hers. His kiss was tinged with desperation as he yanked the hem of her shirt up. Backing her against a tree, he pushed his tongue past her lips and tasted her over and over, more frantic with each stroke. And she understood now. He said so much with the urgency of his touch. He was a confident man—fearless even—but back there, he'd been shaken. He'd been worried about her, and this was him soothing that unfamiliar discomfort. This was him assuring himself she was okay.

His hand cupped her breast, and she arched back with a moan. She wanted him, too. Needed him to put the vision of that massive bear out of her mind. Titus had come after them and for what? He had plenty of fish. Whatever Jenner knew about that bear had upset him, and dammit, she wanted him back—her immovable Jenner.

Lena shoved his shirt upward, and Jenner helped, pulling it off and throwing it to the ground, and then he was back on her, fingers frantic as he pulled off her shirt. His hands were everywhere, creating fire with his touch, heating her to her middle. Fevered and needy for him, she angled her head to give him more access as he trailed biting kisses down her throat.

"Jenner, please," she whispered.

"Fuck," he gritted out, shoving her pants down her hips. "Lena, I'm sorry."

"Don't. I'm not."

When he lifted his eyes to hers, she could see it there. His eyes were dark as pitch now, and it would've scared her if he didn't look so vulnerable. Wild Jenner. Lena leaned forward and bit his bottom lip, then turned and gave him her back.

Jenner let off a long, shaky exhalation, and gripped her waist, drawing her ass against him. "What are you doing?"

"Giving you what you want." Because this was what she wanted, too. She wanted Jenner to take her like he wanted— like he *needed*—right now.

Jenner's lips were on her shoulder and she heard it—the jingle of his pants and the rip of his zipper, and suddenly she was filled with such anticipation, she couldn't stand it. She bowed back against him. Jenner responded with a deep, rumbling growl, and she smiled. She'd done that.

Jenner yanked her hips back and slid into her from behind. He'd said she would be sore from last night, but she wasn't. Or perhaps the pleasure of him filling her outweighed any pain. He bucked deep into her, and unable to hold his weight, she rested against the smooth bark of the birch tree in front of her. He eased out and slammed into her again, his powerful hips thrusting faster. Jenner's arm wrapped around her middle, shielding her from the tree as he cupped her breast, and now his teeth grazed her shoulder blade. "Tell me not to bite you."

"Why?"

Another snarl rattled against her back. "Because you own me woman. Tell me."

"Bite me." It was something he needed, and even if she didn't understand it, she was lost to lust right now. Jenner was wrong. He was the one who owned her.

Jenner slid into her again. "Lena," he gritted out.

He was slamming into her now, so deep, so fast, building pressure until she was blinded with how good he felt when he lost control. He was showing her what he was really like. His feral side, and she fucking loved it. Loved him. Loved every single thing about him.

"Do it," she whispered.

Jenner's teeth sank into her shoulder just as her orgasm throbbed through her. It was quick, and she gasped out at the pain, but the pleasure in her middle was greater. It was bigger, spreading through her as she pulsed hard around his swollen cock. Jenner bucked into her again and went rigid against her back, yelling out her name, and then he pressed his forehead against her hair.

His seed flooded her in hot jets, filling her until it streamed down her thighs as he slid erratically into her.

Jenner's breath was ragged against her hair, but his hands had turned soft, brushing up and down her ribs as his pace slowed and eventually stopped. In a whisper against her ear, he said, "I don't like you out here where you can get hurt. If anything happened to you... Lena, you're important to me. I feel..."

Lena lifted his hand from her breast and kissed his palm. "Me, too."

Jenner let off a long sigh and ran a light touch over the sore spot on her shoulder. "Maybe you won't scar. I didn't go deep."

"What does it mean?"

Jenner swallowed audibly. "It means you're mine."

She smiled off into the dark woods. "Then I hope it scars."

Jenner slid out of her and turned her slowly in his arms, then did something he'd never done before. He hugged her. Just wrapped her up in his strong arms and rocked them slowly back and forth. "Tomorrow, I'll take you to a cabin I know about," he murmured. "You'll sleep in a proper bed, and I'll take better care of you."

"But—"

"Woman, I know this is what you signed up for, and I know you can sleep rough. You're the toughest person I've ever met. It's me. I have this need to put you somewhere safe for a night and give my instincts a rest, okay?"

She nodded, her cheek pressed against his warm chest. "All right."

"Titus is a roamer. I think we are out of his way, but tomorrow will be different. I'll take you to another spot a couple of young bears have been hanging out at." Jenner's lips pressed against the top of her head, lingered there. "We'll get you all the pictures you want, but we have to do it differently than this. I can't protect you like I need to out here. A rifle is no match for bears like Titus, Lena. He'll have you half-devoured before he feels any pain."

"Maybe he was just after those other bears. Maybe one of them was in heat or something."

Jenner shook his head and huffed a humorless laugh. Easing back, he lifted her palm to the half-healed red slash marks she'd nursed the first night she'd met him. She winced at how much it must still hurt him.

"Lena, Titus is a man-eater. We've had three hikers go missing in the last few weeks, and I'd bet everything I own if you opened up that bruin's guts, you'd find them. He has a taste for people. I had plans on coming out here and putting him down, but I can't with you here."

"Because I don't want you to shoot the bears? If he's a man-eater, I understand the necessity."

"A rifle won't be the end of him."

"Then what will?"

"Me."

"I don't understand," she whispered.

Jenner looked sick as he rolled his eyes closed and sighed. "I need to tell you something. I *need* to but I can't."

"Why not?"

He opened those dark eyes, the ones that looked so out of place on his face. His voice dipped to almost nothing. "Because you'll run."

Up on her tiptoes, she wrapped her arms around his shoulders and hugged him tightly. She understood his want to hide the darkest parts of himself. She'd been hiding for years. "I won't run, Jenner. I promise. Just tell me. Say it and let me in."

His heartbeat was pounding against her.

"Please, Jenner."

He hugged her tighter to him and whispered, "I'm a bear."

Lena pursed her lips and stared at the moon through the tree branches over Jenner's shoulder. Whatever she'd expected him to admit to her, that was not it. "Like a bear of a man?"

"No, I mean I'm a bear. Shifter. I'm both. A man and a bear. Shit."

"Soooo...you're saying you can turn into a bear. Like Titus. Furry with teeth and claws."

"Yes."

Lena pushed off him and stood at an arm's length distance because she couldn't hug him while he was saying such ridiculous nonsense. "You're telling me you are a werebear."

"No, a bear shifter."

She blinked slowly and pursed her lips. Okay, sure that explained why he would be so growly, and maybe it even explained his changing eye color. And now his ridiculously heightened sense of smell was making more sense. "You bit me."

"You told me to."

"Am I a bear shifter now, too? Like with a werewolf? You bit me and now I'm a bear? Is that what you're telling me?"

"What? No. Biting doesn't Turn a person into a shifter. At least that doesn't work for bears and werewolves. Other shifters have different abilities."

"I was being sarcastic about werewolves, Jenner! There are werewolves now, too?"

"Yes." He cleared his throat. "You've met some."

Lena just stared. What else could she do? Jenner was the king of la-la land right now.

"Dalton and Chance are—"

"Don't you even say werewolves to me right now, Jenner Silver. If you wanted to play a prank on me, you could've chosen better timing. For example, not right after you fucked me." Lena dressed in a hurry, then turned and stormed off toward a pile of supplies. Oh yes, she was going to build the shit out of the tent, zip herself inside, and wrap her head around the douchebaggery that Jenner had just pulled. With a pathetic little snarl, she dumped the tent out of its storage bag and began spreading it out.

"You're mad."

"Damn straight, I'm mad! I thought you were going to be serious, Jenner! I thought you were going to open up to me. I hope to God you don't actually think you can turn into a bear. I fell for you! I did! And now the words that are coming from your mouth are insane. You get that, right? That what you're saying isn't real?"

Jenner hooked his hands on his hips and arched a dark eyebrow. "Do you want me to Change so you can see I'm not making this up?"

"Sure, Jenner," she muttered, driving a tent stake into the ground. "Turn into a werebear."

"It's just a bear."

"Whatever."

143

"I won't hurt you so don't take off running. It gets my instincts all kicked up when I see something running."

Lena rolled her eyes and moved to the next tent stake. "Don't worry. I won't. And don't be growling and clawing up your hands trying to scare me either, Jenner, or I'm going to kick you right in the dick." Silence. "Jenner?"

"I'm here." The jingling of his pants sounded, and she cast him a pissed-off glare over her shoulder. It was getting darker by the minute, but she could definitely make him out as he undressed.

"Are you serious right now?"

Jenner cracked an obnoxious grin, straight teeth white against the shadows. "I don't want to rip my pants when I let my grizzly out."

"Oh, naturally," she muttered, returning her attention to the next stake. She couldn't freaking wait until she was inside so she could scream into her sleeping bag and draw mustaches and wonky eyes all over her last sketch of him.

"You should know I've never shown Bear to anyone but my brothers."

With an irritated sigh, Lena stood and crossed her arms over her chest. "You call yourself Bear?"

Jenner's irritating smile still lingered at the corners of his lips, and she wanted to claw it right off his stupid face right now. This wasn't funny. Not even close.

"I do because that's what he is. Are you ready?"

"For you to wiggle around and pretend to turn into a bear? This is all of my dreams about my perfect man culminated into one moment, Jenner, so yes, I'm ready."

Jenner hunched forward, but relaxed again and said, "First, I should set some ground rules."

"Are you fucking kidding me? Okay, what?"

"One, I was serious when I said you shouldn't run. Bear likes to chase critters that give him their backs. It's instinct."

"Fine. Check. Go."

"Two, no shooting at me."

"Why would I shoot at you? The gun isn't even anywhere near me. It's still in the saddle you pulled off your horse you dumbass—"

"Whoa, okay, but just the same, don't shoot me."

"Fine! Can we get this pantomime over with, please?"

"Are you in a rush to get somewhere?" he asked, eyebrows high and eyes dancing.

"Yeah, for you to cook my fucking dinner, Jenner. I'm hungry and irritated, and I'm about five seconds away from breaking rule number two. Now shimmy!"

A snap echoed through the woods, and she hunched down, scanning the immediate area. "What was that?"

Three more rattling pops sounded, but it was throatier than a twig breaking. "Jenner," she whispered, heart hammering against her sternum as she turned in a slow circle.

Another volley of pops sounded, but now the air was growing heavy and too thick to breath. A great weight settled across her shoulders and fear nearly froze her in place as she slowly turned her attention onto Jenner. She didn't understand what she saw. He was hunched forward, heaving breath, but with each inhalation, he jerked and grew bigger. And bigger and bigger until he threw his head back with another pop.

Breaking bones. The sound was breaking bones. Lena clapped her hands over her mouth as she arched her gaze up and up, following Jenner's transformation. Tears stung her eyes as fur that shone silver in the evening light covered his skin in a wave. Eight-inch white claws shot from his fingers, and his mouth elongated as curved, razor sharp teeth replaced his own. In the span of a few seconds, it was done, and Jenner stood on his hind legs and rattled off a long growl. That sound—as familiar as her own heartbeat by now because it had been constant since she'd met him. His eyes were dark brown, and so familiar still, but she didn't know this Jenner. This Jenner was massive, as big as Titus, and now he was stalking closer to her, dragging his weapon-like claws through the earth with each powerful stride.

Don't run!

Jenner hadn't lied. He hadn't been teasing her or making something up to push her away.

Jenner was a damned werebear! Bear shifter! Bear! Whatever!

Lena closed her eyes as he came within clawing distance of her. She sure knew how to pick them. Adam had broken her, and now she'd given her heart to a man who was going to eat her. She hoped he choked on her.

She squealed a high pitched, terrified sound as Jenner…er…Bear…snuffled her stomach. But when seconds dragged by, and he just rested his head there, waiting, she cracked one eye open and whispered, "Good Bear. Don't eat me. I'm tough and my bones splinter easily and I taste like piss and gristle."

Bear huffed a breath, and if she wasn't mistaken, it sounded the equivalent to a laugh.

"I'm going to pet you. Yep." She reached out, hands shaking badly. "I'm really going to touch you," she warned, closing her eyes again. She squealed again as her fingers brushed his coarse fur right by his ear.

Bear rubbed his head against her, and she yanked her hand back again, thinking he didn't like it, but no. Apparently Jenner's giant fucking *grizzly bear* was a snuggler. And now there was a humming in his throat she didn't recognize. Was he purring? She touched him again, just a quick pet, there and gone, and since he still didn't seem inclined to devour her and pick his teeth with her bones, she ran her palm over the top of his enormous head.

His body was overwhelmingly enormous and blocked out the entire forest behind him. The muscular hump over his shoulders was taller than she was and, intimidated all over again, she began serial petting him in jerky strokes, trying to stifle the whimper in her throat. At this rate, if her heart beat any faster, it would just explode in her chest, and she would drop like a log.

Bear, apparently sensing her distress because clearly he could sense everything, eased off her and plopped down to the ground where he rolled to his back and wiggled this way and that until the dirt kicked up and made her cough a laugh.

He reached out for her with one giant paw roughly the size of her head.

"Belly scratch?" she asked in a pitch one decibel down from dog whistle.

He huffed a hard breath and wiggled closer, looking more like a giant corgi begging belly rubs than a murderous brown bear.

Lena let off a surprised laugh and stumbled forward on legs that had gone numb and noodle-like. "Right, I'm going to pet your belly now, you massive grizzly." This was not where she imagined her life would end up.

Primly and carefully, she bent at the waist and reached out for him, standing as far away as possible. Bear had a different idea, though, because he curved his paw around her backside and pulled her forward until she fell onto his belly. There she froze, waiting for him to murder her, but nope, he just made the purring noise as she lay like a star on top of him.

"I'm going to make a fur angel," she said in a muffled voice against his belly.

Another Bear laugh, and she was off, arms waving slowly against his massive shape. Her emotions were all over the place as she laughed. Spinning slowly, she slid down his belly and sat on the ground against him.

"This is an awful big secret to keep all this time, Jenner," she whispered, wiping her clammy palms onto her jeans.

Bear curled protectively around her and lay his enormous head next to her, then sighed a sad sound, kicking up dirt again.

"This is why you can growl and your eyes change colors. This is why you can smell everything. I'm sorry I didn't believe you, but you have to understand this isn't in the realm of what I thought could possibly be reality for anyone."

Bear grunted an understanding sound, and she scooted over, snuggling against his neck.

"This is why you and your brothers can't get along." God, what a hard life, keeping a massive beast tucked away. No wonder he preferred to be out here in the wilderness. He'd found the perfect job. As a guide, he only had to deal with people for a short amount of time, and he had the excuse to be scouting when his animal needed to roam. This was the perfect way to make a living for a bear-man like Jenner. And no wonder he was so good at guiding—so sought after. He could find game because he was a freaking bear. He was one of the animals that belonged out in these woods.

Lena inhaled his scent and committed it to memory. Jenner the man had always had a distinct scent of pine, soap, and something she hadn't been able to put her finger on, but now she realized it was this. Animal fur. And as she snuggled closer to him, burying her face against his neck, she fell for him even harder. There were no barriers here in the evening shadows, out here away from anything or anyone that would judge her relationship with a wild man like him. Here, she was safe with her bear-man and could say anything she wanted because no one could hear her but him, and he couldn't respond to reject her. Not like this. Not in bear form.

"Jenner?" He snaked his face closer to her in the dirt, so she dipped her lips near his ear and whispered, "I'm not running. I like you more because you shared this part of yourself with me. I..." She swallowed hard and closed her eyes tightly as she said the words that had been murmuring through her mind. "I love you just the same, maybe more now."

Jenner froze under her, and for a moment, she thought she'd been wrong. Jenner didn't need words to reject her. But as the first tendrils of regret unfurled in her chest, Jenner pulled her closer with his massive arm, his claws gentle against her fragile, paper-thin skin, and his satisfied hum was back in his chest, rattling against her.

And it was enough.

Even if Jenner the man couldn't say the words or perhaps didn't feel as deeply as she did yet, Bear adored her just fine.

TEN

Jenner couldn't take his eyes off her. Her. His mate. Lena didn't understand the mark he'd put on her shoulder yet, but she would. He just had to find the right time to tell her.

Across the fire, Lena had that absent smile that was so fucking adorable he wanted to take her in the tent and make her gasp his name. She was noisy when she came. Perfect. Perfect mate. Telling him just what she liked and training him to understand her body. He'd never felt so deeply about anyone. Not even Brea could touch what was forming between him and Lena.

"Tell me what you're thinking about," she said softly. She hadn't said much since he'd Changed back, but it wasn't the bad kind of silence. The smile on her lips had been constant since he'd come out of the woods a man again, and he'd held her as long as she let him. Until her stomach growled, and his inner bear snarled that he needed to feed her. That he needed to take better care of his mate.

"You," he said simply.

"Oh yeah? Well I'm thinking about me, too, like, I want you to meet my family, and I'm already thinking of excuses for your growls and changing eyes."

"You want me to meet your family?"

Now that blush was back in her cheeks as she dropped her gaze to the fire. "Does that bother you?"

"Bother me? Hell no." It would have to be in the summer, though, and not this year. It was the end of July, and he had two months until hibernation, three max. He was homebound until April because he couldn't risk falling asleep for the winter without a den and where he could be caught. "I like that you've already met one of my brothers."

"About Tobias. You said he scarred you up, but I didn't understand how. He's a bear shifter too, isn't he?"

Jenner nodded once. "We were sixteen and on one of our first Changes, out in the woods and alone and didn't know what was happening."

"Why didn't you know what was happening?"

"Uh, my dad is a bear shifter. All of the men in my lineage are, but unfortunately, Dad wasn't too keen on explaining what we would be going through when we came of age. He was more of a hands-off parent. He thinks that good bear shifters just know how to handle themselves because of instinct."

"But you didn't?"

Jenner shook his head and set his plate down, then stood and walked around the fire just to be closer to her. He couldn't stand not touching her right now. Not after today's close encounter with Titus. Not after what he'd shared with her. Lena hadn't run, and that thought still shocked him. Lena was still here, looking at him like he was a man and not a freak.

Tough woman. His tough woman.

Jenner sat behind her and hugged her back to his chest, rested his chin on the shoulder he hadn't injured. "It was snowing really hard, and Tobias didn't have control of his bear like Ian and I did. He needed to bleed something, and I got in the way, and after he left, I thought I was going to die out there. Ian looked so scared. There was red snow all under me, and I got so cold. All he had was this damned tiny first aid kit. I heal fast thanks to the bear, but he just kept packing snow into my cuts, and he was crying. We were under this little rock ledge, unprotected, and terrified Tobias would come back and finish us both off."

"Oh, Jenner." Heartbreak tainted her soft words.

"We went to battle that spring, and that was the last time we spent any long amount of time together. Our bears are all dominant and can't stand to be close to another bruin. It's the way of it for most of our kind."

"Are there lots of you?"

"No. Hardly any."

"Why?"

Jenner pressed his lips against her temple and frowned at the firelight. He couldn't bring himself to tell her about hibernation right now. Cowardly? Hell yeah, but he just couldn't. Even if Bear wasn't a deal breaker for her, no woman was going to put up with him falling asleep for six months of the year. It wouldn't be fair to ask anyone to stick around for that. So instead he said simply, "We don't pair up easily."

"But your dad did," she argued.

"Nah, he didn't. He got a woman pregnant, never explained what he was, and she was out on raising me and my brothers while we were still in diapers. Bear shifters are not adept at keeping a mate happy."

"A mate," she whispered.

He smiled at how sweetly she'd uttered that word, as if it was something she wanted. She didn't know all of the grit yet, but damn, he would go to his grave remembering just how she'd said that.

"So Dalton and Chance, huh. Owooooo!"

He chuckled and rubbed his cheek against hers. That was the type of affection Bear had been pushing him to give her all along, and now he could finally do it. "Now you get the Wolf Camp reference, right?"

Lena gasped and grinned at him. "Are they going to be pissed that you told me?"

"No, because you aren't going to tell anyone that you know. I mean, no one can know, Lena, or it puts me and my brothers in danger. It puts all shifters in danger. We're really careful with who we tell. Mate's only. It's one of the rules."

"I knew it! Jenner!" Lena twisted in his arms and leveled him with those beautiful honey eyes of hers. "I'm your mate, and you're my mate, right? That's why this feels so big. I mean, from the first time I saw you, you felt important. Like a piece of me had always been tethered to you, and it was a relief just being around you."

God, perfect. She'd just described what he'd felt so adequately. "Yeah."

Her eyes went wide, and the smile dipped from her face. "Is that why you wanted to bite me?"

Jenner pulled the neck of her sweater over to expose the bandage he'd put on her before he'd cooked dinner. "I've never wanted to do that to anyone before."

"Not even Brea?"

He shook his head. "It's called a claiming mark. For shifters, it means you're off limits."

"I'm claimed," she said on a breath as she rested back against him. "By you."

"I thought you would be freaking out more by all of this."

"I should be. This is insane. You have a bear in you, Jenner. Like a giant, sharp-toothed, long-clawed grizzly bear. It's not wrong to still want you, right?"

A laugh rattled his chest, and the stretch of his smile felt so damned good. "I don't think so. You won't be fooling around with my animal or anything. That's taboo in both of our cultures. So no, falling for me isn't wrong." He rocked her to the side and nipped on her neck. "You'll have the man. The bear is just an unfortunate bonus."

"Don't say that. Bear isn't unfortunate. He's a part of you, and I love everything about you." Her voice dipped to nothing at the end. "Sorry."

"For what? Accepting all of me. Yes, woman, I'm offended."

"No, not just for that. I mean, I'm sorry I didn't believe you, and then I'm sorry I said the L-word while you were a bear. I know it's too soon."

"I'm not sorry," he murmured over the crackling fire. He couldn't bring himself to say those words to her until she knew everything, but down to his bones, he felt them. He loved her so deeply it socked him in the gut to think of her leaving, but that was their reality. She had a life and a career that required her to travel, and he was anchored to Alaska, just waiting and preparing to hibernate every year. He wouldn't ever ask her to give that up, and admitting he loved her out loud would be a gateway conversation to doing just that.

Lena deserved a better life than what he could give her.

Swallowing down the snarl of his bear as the beast disagreed, he kissed Lena's lips softly, just as she deserved after all she'd gone through today, then pulled her up. "Off to bed, woman. We have a big day tomorrow."

"More bears?"

He nodded and said, "I'll find you more bears, but this time we'll be safer about it."

"Will you sleep beside me?"

Damn she was so beautiful. Straight-backed with confidence, her long dark hair hanging in waves down her shoulders. And those eyes—such a strange, soft brown color, like she hid an animal within her, too. His mate looked otherworldly as she stood against the flickering firelight, asking him to sleep beside her. Beyond all reason, she still felt safe around him. But she wasn't. Not yet.

"Not tonight." He brushed a soft wave behind her ear just to see her beautiful face better. "I'll keep watch and wake you in the morning."

He wouldn't tell her that he would be hunting Titus tonight.

Lena didn't need the stress of being left alone while he made these woods safer for her.

ELEVEN

Lena startled awake and, for a moment, couldn't remember where she was. She'd been having a good dream that was just on the edge of her memory, so why did she feel so unsettled now?

A soft rustling sound pricked up the fine hairs on her body, and she pursed her lips to try and steady her shaking breath. It was dark, but outside the tent, the embers from the earlier fire still cast the tent in a soft glow.

Some distance off, the horses were restless, pawing the ground and snorting. One let off a whicker, but it sounded terrified, and suddenly, she could make out pounding hooves, as if they'd pulled off their line. Shit.

"Jenner?" she whispered, sitting up in the sleeping bag. Maybe he was Changed into his bear and stressing out the horses.

A massive shadow covered the tent and then disappeared. *Oh God, please let that be Jenner!*

As quietly as she was able, Lena reached over and pulled the long knife she carried in a sheath on her belt. It wouldn't do jack shit against a pissed off grizzly, but if she went for the eyes, maybe she could buy herself time.

The shadow moved around the tent, disappearing into the darkness in the back and reappearing on the side that glowed with firelight. A short bellow blasted from the animal, jolting fear through her. Not Jenner. That didn't sound anything like him, and there was nothing in between her and whatever bear was out there save the thin nylon of the tent.

The animal snuffled against the bottom edge of the flimsy shelter. Against the fabric, she could make out the outline of a brown bear's massive nose. Lena clutched the knife tighter and held her breath. Where the fuck was Jenner?

The bear stood up on its hind legs, and this was it. In a rush, she pulled her backpack in front of her just as the beast dropped down and raked its claws down the tent, shredding it.

"Jenner!" she screamed as a massive claw ran down the backpack and yanked it from her grasp.

Through the tattered tent, she could see him now. Dark brown bear, scarred neck, missing ear. Titus.

She couldn't escape the tent to run because the bruin was blocking the only exit, and as he pulled the backpack out, he clamped his massive jaws around it and shook the thing, scattering everything from it. The power of his jaws had tears streaming down the sides of her face in terror. With a bellowing roar, the monster turned his attention to her, so close she could see one of his eyes was fogged with blue. She scrambled for that side of him, hoping to confuse him, but he was on her now. She could see it the second he swung his head toward her and locked his gaze on hers. Shoving forward, he stretched his claws through the opening and just as he reached her, she slammed the blade of her knife as hard as she could into his arm.

The bear jerked back and bellowed an awful sound. Anger and pain. And right as he pushed forward again, tilting the entire tent with him, something hit him on his side with the force of a meteor.

Jenner! The sound of their brawling was overwhelming, hurting her ears with the sheer volume. And when she stumbled out of the collapsing tent, she couldn't comprehend the raw violence of the enormous grizzlies. Titus slammed into a tree, and it snapped in two with an echoing crack.

Jenner was much lighter in color and easy to tell apart, but now he was being clawed and bitten. Titus latched his teeth onto Jenner's neck and shook him.

"Oh my gosh, oh my gosh," she chanted as she bolted for the rifle. This couldn't be happening!

Fingers fumbling, she pulled the snap on the saddle and yanked the rifle. She shoved a bullet in the chamber and pulled it to her shoulder. Tight, just like Dad taught her. Aim. Steady. Slow breaths, one, two, hold on the third. Shit! Jenner and Titus were just a mass of fur and teeth as they warred in the dim glow of the smoldering fire. She didn't want to hit Jenner. Couldn't hit him. She loved him.

They weren't disconnecting at all, latched onto each other as they fought to the death.

Jenner ghosted her a look and let off a growl. What kind of directions was he giving her? Shoot? Shoot now?

He spun around and slammed Titus to the ground so this must be it. The chance he was giving her, the clear shot. With trembling hands, she lifted the scope and wished to God there was more light than this. She zeroed in on Titus, but just as she pulled the trigger, Jenner let off a frantic snarl. She jerked the gun a millimeter as she brushed the trigger and suddenly, Titus went mad. Snarling, roaring, charging toward her. She whimpered and chambered another round, but he was coming too fast. Just a few yards before he reached her, Jenner pulled down the man-eater's back end, slamming him to the ground. And with a sob, Lena pulled the trigger again.

And this time, she didn't miss.

Titus went limp and let off a long breath—his last. The fury in his eyes glazed over to emptiness as the rifle sagged in Lena's arms. Desperate to get away from him, she staggered backward and clicked the safety on.

Jenner was glaring at her, his body heaving with breath and his fur matted with red. Sure, Titus looked worse off, but Jenner was hurt.

He paced behind Titus, his fevered eyes on her.

"What? You said shoot!" At least she thought he did.

Jenner let off a pissed roar and disappeared into the woods behind him. And when he came back, naked and dripping crimson from slash marks across his torso, the anger in his eyes hadn't dimmed one bit. "I meant run, not shoot, Lena! For fuck's sake, you could've been killed!"

Her mouth dropped open as anger rippled through her body. "You're damn right I could've been killed. I was practically a burrito in that tent when he attacked, Jenner! Where were you?"

Jenner opened his mouth, then closed it again. He narrowed his eyes and hooked his hands on his bare hips. He jammed a finger at the limp grizzly. "I was hunting *him*."

"Yeah, well you didn't have to because he was hunting us first! And you're welcome!"

She pushed the gun back into its holder and stormed off to clean up all of her belongings strewn around camp. And now she was crying harder. Not only was she scared half to death by what had just happened, but she was dealing with Jenner's anger on top of that.

"Hey," he said, hand on her shoulder as he pulled her around. He hugged her close and whispered, "Shhhh," as she really broke down.

"I don't understand bear-growls, Jenner. You backed off Titus, and I thought you were giving me room to shoot."

"And you did so fucking good. You were a warrior. I mean, yeah, most people's instinct would be to run—"

"But he was hurting you."

Jenner huffed a laugh and turned his head, staring at Titus's still form. With a long sigh, he murmured, "Woman, you're terrifying."

"I'm terrifying? I just saved your ass."

"And you broke rule number two."

"Rule number—" She squinted and tried to remember what he'd said, and when it dawned on her, she jerked back. "I shot you? Where?" She was shrieking again.

"It's not bad," he muttered, pulling his arm in for a better look and, son of a cock-chafer, sure enough, there was a hole in his bicep, bleeding freely.

"Ooooh," she said, fluttering her fingers over the injury helplessly. "I didn't mean to do that, but you shouldn't have growled at me and distracted me in the first place. I had a good shot." She crossed her arms over her chest and glared. "You practically shot yourself."

Jenner reared back like she'd just thrown cold water on him, but humor swam in his still dark eyes. "Are you blaming this on me? Seriously?"

Primly, she lifted her chin. "I'm sorry I shot you."

"I give you two damn rules to follow, and you break one less than four hours after I laid them down," he grumbled, making his way toward the first aid kit, which was currently lying by the fire, wide open with its contents scattered across the ground.

He bent down, long, powerful legs folding beneath him, and picked up a package of bandages. "Would you mind?"

"That is not enough for all of"—she waved her hand at the gore on his torso—"that."

"These will be fine. The bullet went straight through and clipped a bone, though, and while it heals, I'd rather not get dirt packed in it."

"Do you get infections?" she asked, a sliver of worry snaking through her.

"No, but it sucks having your body push dirt out of you slowly."

"Oh." Lena cleaned it as best as she could with what little supplies were still intact, and when she pulled the gauze tight around the clean bandage, she felt like grit. Jenner was trying to hide it from her, but he was hurting. Without a word, he turned from the embers and picked up Titus's back leg, then dragged him off into the woods like the massive grizzly weighed nothing.

Lena stood there in shock as he disappeared into the trees. Jenner was a lot stronger than he'd ever let on, and as she looked down at her hands, sticky with his blood, everything that had happened over the past couple of days crashed over her like a tidal wave.

Losing her virginity, the bears at the river, running from Titus, Jenner's bite, finding out the man she loved was a freaking bear shifter, and now this? Being attacked by a man-eater that had likely eaten hikers and watching Jenner battle with him. Killing it. Hurting Jenner. She gasped and wiped her hands across her jeans over and over, trying desperately to get the red off her palms. Titus had been hunting them since last night, hell-bent on *killing* her. She'd almost died just now.

The shaking started in her hands, and a cold tingling sensation traveled up her limbs and landed in her middle. She was going to throw up or pass out, or maybe both. What was that grating sound?

"Lena?" Jenner said, hands out like he was calming a startled colt. Where had he come from?

The sound picked up, and she was truly surprised to find it was coming from her. She was sobbing, shoulders shaking with each pathetic cry that wrenched from her raw throat. Jenner had his jeans on now, and the claw marks on his chest had stopped bleeding. How long had she been like this? Minutes? An hour?

"He…was going…to *eat* me," she said, her voice completely unrecognizable and punctuated by hysterical hiccups.

"No, he wouldn't have because I wouldn't let that happen. I had you. I heard you call for me, and I was already coming for you."

"I have blood on my hands," she said, looking down at the smeared red. Two tears made tiny splats on her palms. "Jenner, I literally have blood on my hands."

"It's okay. It's just mine." That made it even worse! Jenner hugged her tightly. "Shhh, you're okay. I'm here. We're both okay."

Swallowing down her weakness, she whispered shakily, "I think I'm in shock."

"I know you are. Your skin is cold as ice."

He rubbed her arms, but she could barely even feel his touch. Everything seemed so surreal, like she was floating in some dreamscape. Through the trees, the dawn was lightening the sky, but she wasn't ready for the world to just spin on like she hadn't almost died in some horrific way.

"Stupid happy sun," she muttered, glaring at the sunrise.

In a confused tone, Jenner asked, "Do you want to go back to sleep?"

"So I can have nightmares about Titus? Hell no. Where are the horses?" The line they'd been tied to was completely empty.

"Uuuh, probably halfway back to the lodge by now."

Her voice jacked up an octave. "We're stranded out here?"

"No. I have a radio up at that hunter's cabin I was telling you about. It's about a five mile walk from here, but we can call up to the lodge for help when we get there."

"Okay, okay," she chanted, bobbing her head. Jenner had a plan. Good. He was capable and strong, and he was a fucking grizzly bear, so she could do this.

Five miles.

After what she'd endured, this would be a piece of cake.

TWELVE

Lena was so damned beautiful it hurt to look away. Which was why Jenner had been sitting in this old creaky chair for the past half an hour watching her sleep.

One more day.

With a regretful sigh, he leaned back in the chair and stretched out his legs. From here, his boot almost touched the cot Lena was sleeping on. The old abandoned cabin was just one small room, and the window near the door had been broken, letting the critters in. Something had made a nest in the corner, and it smelled like animal urine, but at least Lena was safe, encased in these thick log walls. And after last night, she needed to feel safe again.

Titus's attack had rattled her badly. Any man with eyes in his head could see she was reeling. And after he'd radioed into the lodge and asked the Dawson cousins to bring them new horses, she'd fallen asleep hard on the cot against the far wall. He didn't blame her. In fact, her body probably needed the sleep to deal and heal.

He couldn't ask her to stay, and now the trip would be cut short and his precious time with her had just been ripped in half. Fuck, why did this hurt so much? Just the thought of losing her was enough to double him over, but this was his reality.

They would ride back with Chance and Dalton, and she would go back to her life soon after. He'd seen the pictures she'd taken yesterday, and they were incredible. She'd gotten the river bears and the two running away from Titus. They looked like two grizzlies charging and were likely a cover shot any outdoor magazine would cut off their fingers to own rights to.

Their belongings were in a messy pile near the front door, and through the broken window, a breeze fluttered the pages of Lena's waterlogged journal. It had been splashed during Titus's attack.

Standing, Jenner checked the bandage on his arm, then strode over to where the journal sat. It was open, and on the page was a picture of himself, casting his glance backward, looking irritated. With a frown, he bent down and opened the journal wider. The sketch was detailed and skilled, but he hated that she saw him cold like this. He flipped a couple of pages, both pictures of bears with notes in the columns, and landed on another picture of himself, walking in front of his horse, mouth open like he was talking to it. He didn't look so unapproachable here.

There were more. One of him on the deck at the lodge, amusement in his eyes. One of him in front of the mirror in his room, claw marks jagged across his ribs. He had his hand out, as if telling her not to come any closer, but his eyes were soft. There was another of him with his back to her, riding his horse on a trail, and all around them were quickly sketched trees with a bald eagle flying overhead, but it was the last one that made him draw up in realization. It was a detailed drawing of him sitting on the other side of the campfire, smiling. He flipped through them again, faster this time. She'd captured actual moments between them, and as he studied the pictures, he could feel her falling in love with him.

Chest aching, he pulled her camera into his lap and sat heavily on the ground. He flipped through the pictures, one by one. She had taken lots of photographs of him when he hadn't been paying attention, and they told a story. They transformed him slowly from a mysterious, cold soul to a warm man. Care had been taken with the last several pictures, and he stopped scrolling on one of him sleeping.

She must've taken it that first morning in the tent when he'd slept through the night beside her. He'd never slept so good in all his life, which made no damned sense because they were out in the wild and his instincts were always on alert.

He wasn't wearing a shirt and was sleeping on his stomach, his cheek resting on his arm and his face completely relaxed.

Jenner turned the camera off and looked up at where Lena lay asleep on the cot.

He'd screwed up.

He'd lost track of why he couldn't make a move on her. Now their separation would hurt them both, and it was all his fault. Dammit, if he'd just kept it professional, he could've stopped the bond. Probably. Or at least he could've hidden it from her if he'd remained aloof like he'd meant to.

But no. Like a rutting animal, he'd given into his wants almost immediately, and then bore his entire freaking bear-tainted soul to her. Now she would leave. She had to. The pictures on her camera would give her huge opportunities in her career, and he couldn't stand in the way of that. Jenner couldn't ask her to be happy with a man who hibernated six months out of the year instead of following her dream.

He loved her enough to want better for her.

One more day, and Lena would leave, and when she did, she would take his heart with her.

****

"I have to take lots of landscape pictures so the art department has options in case they want to put an animal into different scenery."

"Mmm," Jenner rumbled distractedly as he skipped another rock across the creek.

He'd been distant all day, and her conversations had turned desperate. She wanted so badly for him to open up again, but whatever Titus's attack had done to her, it had locked Jenner up completely.

Jenner frowned off into the woods, then back at the cabin that was barely visible through the trees. "I tracked down my mom."

Lena stopped taking pictures and let the camera rest against her chest. "What? When?"

"Five years ago. I never told my brothers."

"Why not?"

"Because I still don't know how I feel about it. I found her in Anchorage. I was too young to remember what she looked like, but apparently she's a big, respected news anchor. I'd been watching her on the news for years and hadn't even known she was my mom." He skipped another

BEAR FUR HIRE | T. S. JOYCE

rock, then sank down onto the gravelly beach, resting his arms on his knees as his eyes got a faraway look. "We met for lunch at this nice restaurant, and I was sure I would feel this connection to her, you know?" Jenner leveled Lena with those vibrant baby blues.

Lena sat beside him and rested her cheek against his arm. "What happened?"

"There was nothing. I didn't know her, and she didn't know me. And she didn't want to. My dad spent a lot of time convincing us that he didn't care that she left. That wasn't true. My dad had tried to make it work with her. Tried to co-parent us. Even thought about telling her what he was and what we would become."

"She didn't know?"

Jenner huffed a breath and shook his head. "Some people can be trusted with this secret. Some can't. Dad was right not to tell her. I can hear a lie, and she was full of half-truths. I thought for a minute she wasn't capable of being genuine, but then she told me the reason she left, and it was the first truly honest thing she said to me. She hadn't wanted the life Dad offered her. It wasn't enough." Jenner rested his cheek against her head. "She hadn't wanted to be a mother, and when she found out she was having triplets, she felt this heaviness, like she couldn't breathe because her life was

177

over. She had big dreams, and living in some cabin out in the middle of nowhere, raising multiples, wasn't what she wanted. She said she tried for the first two years, but every day she woke up feeling like she was drowning. And then she told me that she was sorry, but she didn't regret her decision because she'd made something of herself."

"Wow, what a horribly shitty mother."

Jenner sighed. "Yeah, her mothering instincts weren't awesome."

"You know she could've chased those dreams and been a parent too, right?"

"Lena, she didn't even know what she was into, though. She had triplets, and that was breaking her. Imagine when she learned we were all bear shifters."

"So what? You change into a bear. You aren't man-eaters. You all have good jobs and good lives. You're all successful. She bailed, Jenner. From age two to when you tracked her down, she had no contact with you, and her excuse was sorry but I'm not sorry? I got the life I wanted and fuck the rest of you?" Lena shook her head, baffled and trying to imagine leaving a child. She couldn't even fathom the pain. Couldn't. "I would never leave a kid."

"And you won't have to be put in the position to choose."

Lena jerked back and frowned up at him. "What do you mean?"

Jenner looked sick right now. "You don't know everything," he whispered. "It's not as simple as me just turning into a bear every once in a while."

"Then tell me."

Jenner gave his attention to the creek, so she shoved his arm. "Don't close down again, Jenner. Tell me. Let me decide if it's too much. Tell me!"

"What's the point? Huh?" he barked, eyes sparking like blue flames. "I didn't tell you that story about my mom to unload on you. I told you so you would understand why I'm doing this."

Lena felt bear-slapped, and for a moment, she couldn't speak. Couldn't breathe. She could only look at the man she loved and realize what this discussion was really about. He wasn't just distancing himself. He was pushing her away. For good. "Doing what?" she whispered. She needed to hear him say it.

"You don't belong here, Lena," he murmured, but his voice sounded strange. Half-truth. "You have this huge career that requires a lot of you. I can't ask you to become stagnant for me."

"Stagnant? Have you looked around, Jenner? There's a fucking porcupine over there." She jammed her finger across the creek at the critter meandering down the bank. "There's a picture. It's not like I would be visiting some high-rise city with nothing but rats to photograph. And you're wrong. I do belong here, or at least in a place like this. I feel at home out in the woods. I always have. I'm not saying I have to move in with you. I can visit or find a place nearby. I mean, I live out of a hotel! My belongings are what I brought with me. I had a pet plant, and it died on my last trip to Montana. I have no roots, and someday I'll want some. This feels big between us, Jenner." She clutched the sleeve of his sweater, desperate to banish his vacant expression. "Look at me! This is big. For you and for me, too, because I haven't felt like this with anyone else."

"You got a broken marriage with Adam, and now you'll have a broken pairing—"

"Don't you even finish that sentence."

"I hibernate, Lena!"

"What?"

Jenner let off a long, shaky breath, and now the emotion in his eyes mirrored hers. "In a couple months, I'll go to sleep, and I won't wake up until April."

Lena gritted her teeth and shook her head slowly back in forth in denial. "No."

Jenner's eyebrow's lifted slightly. "Yes. Every year it happens. There's no way to stop it. I've fucking tried! I can't stay awake. Every winter, I pick a different den somewhere around here and hope hunters don't stumble onto it while I'm asleep. That's the reality of this life."

"But...your brother is married."

"Yeah, and Elyse is different. She's tough as leather and a homesteader, born and raised in Alaska and more adept at dealing with her mate sleeping half the fucking year. And it's hard on her, Lena. She's scarred now from protecting Ian last winter. Do you want Elyse's life? Really? When you imagine giving up your career for a man, do you imagine spending six snowy months trapped in a small house fighting cabin fever all alone? I don't want that for you. Can't you see?" Moisture rimmed his eyes, and through gritted teeth, he said, "I want better. I want you happy, and what I am will steal your happiness. I can't do it." Jenner stood and strode off toward the cabin. "I won't."

A sob left her lips as she watched him go. Hibernation? What a mess of a life. Half of his time was spent completely unconscious, and suddenly it made perfect sense why he wasn't married with kids already. Because before, it didn't.

It didn't make a damned lick of sense why he'd chosen her to give his attention to, but here was the rub. She could fuck him for a few days, but Jenner, in reality, was untouchable. She hadn't really ever stood a chance at keeping him because his secrets were too big, and too dark.

She doubled over the pain in her middle. How could something hurt so badly? She'd been right to avoid attachment to people all this time because this was agony.

"Lena?" Dalton said in a soft voice. "Are you okay?"

Tears streaming, she looked up at the dark-haired man who stood near her with worry in his charcoal black eyes. Behind him, Chance stood, holding the reins of two horses, shifting his weight from side to side, clearly uncomfortable with the tsunami of emotion washing through Lena right now.

Jenner had timed it just perfectly, hadn't he? Break her heart right before the Dawsons showed up. Right before the long ride to the lodge so she could wrap her head around the fact that the man she adored wouldn't be in her life any longer. Just like Adam all over again.

"I should've listened to you," she said, clutching her stomach.

"Shhh," Dalton said, gripping her shoulder.

"Ow," she gasped, jerking out from under his hand.

Dalton's eyes narrowed, and he pulled her forward, yanking the neck of her shirt back to expose the bandage. "Please tell me that's not what it looks like," he growled out. He rounded on Jenner, who was packing the saddle bags of a black horse. "Please fucking tell me you didn't claim her!" His voice snapped with fury, and a long, low snarl sounded from Chance.

Jenner ignored them both.

"Did you tell her what it means?"

"He did, and you don't have to worry. All of the secrets here will go with me to my grave. And relax, Dalton," she said, standing. She hoisted herself over the saddle of a bay. "Jenner's bite is just a bite and nothing more. It didn't stick." She nudged her horse and guided him toward the trail they had come in on.

Hoofbeats sounded moments later, and Dalton pulled up beside her. "That's not how it works, Lena. If his bear chose you, you're it for always."

"Yeah, well, he's decided I don't belong out here."

"You don't! God dammit, Jenner," Dalton yelled, twisting in the saddle to where Chance and Jenner followed on their own mounts.

Jenner's eyes were now the color of midnight, though, and a long snarl rattled from his chest. His horse skittered to the side and blasted a snort. "Careful, dog. This doesn't concern you."

Dalton huffed a disgusted sound and kicked his horse into a trot.

Lena followed, urging her horse faster. The quicker they made it back to the lodge, the quicker she could escape the anguish of being too close, yet too far away from Jenner.

THIRTEEN

"You okay?" Dalton asked for the billionth time since they'd left the cabin.

Chance and Jenner were far behind, lagging and talking too low for her to hear.

"I'm fine."

"I can see in the dark really well, so we don't have to stop until we get to the lodge."

"Dalton? Why do you care so much about what is going on with Jenner and me?"

He looked at her for a long time, his face cast in blue light from the moon above. "Because I hurt a girl once trying to settle down. I don't want that for you."

"So, it's not because you like me?"

"I like you fine, but not in the way you think. I mean, sure, I like giving Jenner shit, but a wise wolf knows better than to mess with a bear's claim."

"But you tried to stop the bond from happening."

"Yeah well, I've seen the aftermath, and it ain't pretty. Not on the woman, and not on the animal. Jenner and I stay at each other's throats, but we've known each other a long time. He's one of my best friends."

"You don't hibernate though, do you? Not like the bear shifters?"

Dalton shook his head but wouldn't meet her gaze anymore.

"So then as far as shifters go, you got lucky."

"Mmm. Depends on how you look at it. Some wolf packs go crazy. The McCalls have to be put down one by one."

"Who does that?"

Dalton jerked his head toward Jenner, who was barely visible so far behind them. "The Silver brothers are the enforcers around here. If a shifter steps out of line, Jenner and his brothers fix the problem."

"What? Why them? That doesn't seem fair. I mean, they have enough shit going on without policing everyone."

"Not everyone. Just the ones who threaten to expose us or who hurt humans. And just in Alaska. The Silvers can handle it, and most of the time, just their presence here keeps the rest of us in line."

"Oh." She relaxed into the gentle rocking gait of her horse. There was so much more to Jenner than she'd known. She couldn't have ever guessed how complicated his life was, and now his story about his mom made more sense. He didn't want her weighed down with his shifter shit for the rest of her life. Still, she wasn't his mother and she deserved to make an educated decision for her own life, not be booted out of his without her consent. "So the McCalls all go crazy?"

"Every one of them. Those boys have poison in their blood. They have a long history as man-eaters. Not like the Dawson pack. Your mate helps keep humans safe from the McCalls."

"My mate," she murmured. Too bad that word didn't mean more to Jenner.

"I can't have daughters," Dalton admitted low. "I mean I can, but they die when they're born. Bears just don't have female offspring. All of their babies live. My woman lost a daughter, and we never recovered. I'll never try again. Hurting a mate, for a shifter, it's the worst feeling in the world. I can see you're pissed at Jenner, but he has his reasons for doing what he's doing. He's feeling this, too, even if he doesn't act like it."

"Oh no, Dalton. I'm so sorry about your daughter."

He twitched his head. "Bears are unlucky with their hibernation, wolves are unlucky with breeding. We get the animals and the power that comes along with them, but we sacrifice other things. We don't settle down easily, you understand? It's not because we don't want to. It's because we don't want to hurt the women we fall for."

"But shouldn't it be up to your mates to decide whether they can handle this life?"

Dalton shrugged one shoulder up to his ear. "I don't know. Before I bonded to my woman, I would've said yes, but looking back now, I should've stopped what was happening between us from the start."

Lena's heart sank at how jaded Dalton's experiences had made him. And she didn't blame him. Losing a child and then separating from a mate were life experiences so unimaginably painful, how could they not change a person's outlook on life?

"I lost my first mate," she said with a sympathetic look. "I totally understand how it changes you."

Dalton looked up at the moon. "We make one hell of a pack out here," he murmured. "All broken."

But he was wrong. They weren't broken. Broken was what happened when they went through something hard and stopped living. Broken was what happened when a person

188

started running and never looked back. She'd done that. She'd been broken, and she saw nothing but strong men here. Their experiences made them tougher, and they were each still trying, even if they'd given up on mates.

This was the first moment in years that she *didn't* feel broken.

And as soon as she got to the lodge, she was going to upload her pictures, send them off to *Bucks and Backwoods* before her deadline, then ask for Tobias to be her bush pilot out of here because it was unacceptable to break all over again.

She'd finally begun to find herself and Jenner had been pivotal in starting the changes in her. She understood his desire for her to live a better life than he thought he could provide, and she loved him even more for it. That was his sacrifice, but now it was her turn.

Lena wasn't ready to give up on this, even if he was.

The beginnings of a plan were forming in her mind, but she needed a Silver brother to help carry it out. Tobias didn't know it yet, but he was about to pay Jenner back for shredding him up all those years ago.

Tobias was about to save them both.

****

Jenner leaned against the kitchen island and stared suspiciously at Lena, who was sitting at the dining table, typing away on her laptop. Was she smiling? This was not how he'd imagined their last morning together. He'd prepared himself for more death-glares and tears, but from the looks of it, Lena was just going to ignore him completely until she left this place in an hour.

And he wasn't the only one who noticed because Dalton and Chance both kept shooting Lena worried looks from the couch where they were talking with their new clients.

Sure, women were confusing as shit, but Jenner was being gutted every minute that drew them closer to goodbye, and Lena had just literally laughed out loud at something she read on her glowing computer screen.

She took another bite of the apology sandwich he'd made her and clicked away on her little laptop mouse. Out of sheer curiosity, he ambled around the other side of the dining table like he was going to join the others, but sat on the back of the couch and looked at what she was doing on her computer instead. She was attaching the pictures to an email from the looks of it.

"You aren't sending pictures of me, are you?"

Lena cast him an angry glare over her shoulder. There it was. "Those are just for me."

Jenner licked his bottom lip and gripped the edge of the leather couch he was resting against. "Do you want to talk in private? About anything? I mean, before you leave do you want to...I don't know...yell at me?"

"Nope."

The pain in his chest intensified, and he stifled a growl because the trio of mid-thirties men on a bachelor party adventure were close enough to hear. And he'd be damned if he outed his beastly nature to humans twice in one week.

Lena's hair was pulled back in a long ponytail, and the lighter auburn ends curled under, showing off that long, pretty neck of hers, but also the top edge of the bandage that sat right under the neck of her shirt.

She was his. *His*, and he was about to let her go. Fuck, he hated this stupid urge to be a decent person. He hated feeling trapped. Wanting her to stay more than anything, but needing to push her to leave and find someone normal. A regular human guy who could be there for her always, not just during the warm season. Who would encourage her drive to be the best in her industry. Who could give her little babies, not cubs, who would grow up to go to college and marry normal women and give Lena normal grandchildren. And he could picture it all. Her hair streaked with silver, glasses on her nose, with a huge family gathered around her for holidays while he would still be here, sleeping through. But as much as he told himself he wanted that for her, he hated the thought of her making a family with anyone else. Of her spending the holidays with another family. And how fucking selfish, right? He hadn't been awake for a Christmas since he was fifteen, but he begrudged her having that with people she could actually celebrate with?

Pushing off the couch, he strode from the cabin and off the porch, then across the massive yard to the deck overlooking the river. He couldn't be in there while she looked so unaffected by all this. He was burning inside, and she couldn't look more relaxed to be leaving him. And yeah, this was his fault—his choice. She'd cried so hard when he'd told her she needed to go and that it wouldn't work out between them, so by God, he thought it would've been harder for her to separate.

He'd been her first.

He'd given her his mark, but maybe that didn't mean as much to her. Maybe humans didn't feel bonds like shifters did. He didn't know. All he knew was that for the first time in his life, he hated what he was because Bear had cost him Lena.

Lena would be it for him. For the rest of his life, he would never want another. His bear had chosen, and now she was an hour away from leaving, and she seemed completely at ease.

"Fuck!" he yelled, chucking a heavy tree branch into the woods.

He was burning alive and she was fine. Smiling. Beautiful, perfect, strong, too good for him, and a panicked part of him wanted to beg her to stay. He wanted to beg her to feel something for him and not flip that switch so easily. Was he really so easy to forget?

He paced in front of the deck, running his hands roughly over his hair.

Lennard had told him "good job." He'd said Lena had filled out a survey first thing this morning and given Jenner all five stars. Called him an "attentive and professional guide," and she would recommend him to anyone. Her answers had been emotionless.

She wasn't fighting this at all, and that fact was relentlessly slicing up his insides until he wanted to Change just to escape these roiling human sentiments.

The scent of dominant grizzly hit his nose an instant before he turned around to find Tobias standing there. A mass of emotions washed over him. His bear wanted to kill him, but the human side of Jenner was relieved to see Tobias after all this time. He hadn't laid eyes on him since Ian and

Elyse's wedding at the beginning of the warm season. And dammit, right now, he needed something. Someone. He needed his brother to tell him it would be okay.

"What have you done?" Tobias asked softly.

"I claimed her." Jenner swallowed and linked his hands behind his head. He nearly choked on the poisonous words as he admitted again, "I claimed her."

He thought Tobias would be pissed. He thought he would want to fight him, bleed him, because that's what Tobias did. His bear was a brawler, but instead, pity and understanding slashed through his brother's green eyes. "You can't keep her, can you?"

Jenner's chin trembled, and he swallowed his emotion down, dragged his gaze to the river so his brother wouldn't see how weak he was. "I can't keep her. She's not even having a hard time leaving me. I picked someone who doesn't feel the same. And it's good, you know? It's good for her to leave but fuck it all, I thought it would be harder on her."

"Like it is on you?"

Jenner nodded and swallowed over and over to keep from retching.

"You marked her?"

"I couldn't help it."

"Shit."

Jenner let off an angry laugh. "Yeah."

Tobias approached and pulled him into a rough hug, shocking Jenner to complete stillness. "I'm sorry brother. I don't envy the hurt you'll feel when she's gone." Tobias clapped him so hard on the back, Jenner's bones rattled, but it wasn't uncomfortable. Jenner gave him a quick hug back before Tobias disengaged. Both of their bears were snarling and enraged, and the pungent stink of dominance was a heavy fog between them, but as Tobias strode for the lodge, Jenner realized this was the first time his brother had embraced him since they were kids. Since before they turned into bears for the first time. Since that first hibernation when Tobias's bear had tried his damndest to kill him.

So there was the silver lining. He would lose his heart when Lena left. He would lose an important piece of himself, but because of his pain, he'd had this profound moment with Tobias. At least there was that.

Jenner took a long, steadying breath, then walked back to the lodge where Lena was saying goodbye to everyone on the front porch. He rested one boot on the bottom stair and waited for her to finish hugging the Dawsons. With a sympathetic look, Tobias strode past him, loaded down with

Lena's belongings, and headed for the runway. Dalton and Chance pulled Lennard inside, leaving him and Lena alone.

"I'm sorry," he said, his voice breaking on the apology.

"Shhh," she said, cupping his cheek.

He leaned into her touch and scraped his three day scruff against her soft palm, reveling in the last touch he would ever have from her.

"Everything will be okay. You'll be okay," she murmured.

The morning sunlight landed in her soft brown eyes, making them look devastatingly beautiful. He couldn't do this. He had to do this. He wanted to roar and claw and keep her here, but he couldn't hurt her life like that.

"Say it before I go," she murmured.

Oh, he knew what she meant. Say the three words he hadn't yet, but that she had gifted him time and time again. "Why?"

"Because I need to hear it, and you need to say it. Because I want to know this wasn't just pretend to you."

He swallowed hard and rasped out, "I love you, Lena."

Lena let off a soft gasp and closed her eyes, as if she'd been waiting for those words all her life. Unable to help himself, Jenner leaned forward and kissed her, and slowly, she softened against him and parted her lips, allowing him to brush his tongue against hers for the last time. Last taste. Last kiss. Not enough.

Lena looked devastated when she pulled away, but instead of saying anything, she handed him an envelope.

"What's this?"

"A tip. You earned it. You saved me in more ways than you know."

Jenner opened it and, sure enough, there was a small stack of twenty dollar bills inside. He shook his head and handed it back to her. "It doesn't feel right taking a tip from you."

"Why not?"

"Because"—he kissed her palm to stall and steady his voice—"you gave me the best days of my life. Can't you see your money will taint that?"

Lena clutched the envelope to her chest and nodded. With a sad smile, she murmured, "Goodbye, Jenner." She brushed past him but not before he saw a single, glistening tear track down her cheek.

She walked toward where Tobias waited on the edge of the woods and didn't look back.

He couldn't do this. Couldn't watch her walk out of his life. His bear shredded his insides as he jogged toward the trees on the opposite side of the clearing. His boots crunched across the earth as he picked up his pace.

He was going to Change, and he didn't want her to see him lose it. Lose her. Lose himself.

Bye, Lena.

****

Lena gasped as the woods shook with a deafening roar. There was such agony in it.

Tobias threw a pitying look to the woods behind them but kept walking.

God, that had been one of the hardest things she'd ever done, pretend to say goodbye to him. But if she told him what she was thinking, he would make a harder run at pushing her away, and she couldn't handle that right now. Not after everything they'd been through.

"Stupid man," she said, wiping her damp cheek on her shoulder.

Tobias didn't say anything, only walked silently beside her, loaded down with all of her luggage.

"Do you think I'm right in leaving?" she asked softly.

"It isn't my place to say."

"I'm asking your honest opinion, Tobias."

A rumbling growl blasted from him, and he rounded on her. "No, all right? I think it's fucked up what you're doing to each other. These kinds of games get people hurt." He glared over her shoulder at the woods behind her. "It'll get my brother hurt."

"Good."

"What?"

"Now you'll help me."

Tobias narrowed his eyes. "Help you how?"

"Help me keep your brother because despite his best efforts and beyond all reason, I love the idiot, and I'm not ready for him to push me away."

Tobias reared back, blinking hard. And then a slow, approving smile took his face. "What do you need me to do?"

"Fly me to Galena." Lena lifted her chin primly. "I want to meet Elyse."

FOURTEEN

Flying in a little bush plane was a lot less terrifying when the weather was fair. This time Lena didn't even scream when Tobias landed the plane on a long, smooth strip outside of the tiny town of Galena, Alaska.

Tobias waved to a man who stood leaned against a muddy green SUV near a pair of covered bush planes. He must've been the one Tobias radioed on the way over here.

"He's your ride to Ian and Elyse's homestead," Tobias explained, his green eyes clear and serious.

"You aren't coming to see your brother? You're so close."

"I'm afraid I can only handle one brother today. Link will get you where you need to go."

Tobias helped her out, unloaded her belongings, and set them in the back of the SUV.

"Lincoln McCall," the tall, lanky man with wild gray eyes introduced himself. His handshake was rough and was punctuated by a long rattling snarl and then a quick hard shake of his head, as if he hadn't meant to let the warning sound slip.

"Link's half-mad already," Tobias said, clapping the man on the back. "Careful not to piss him off, yeah?"

"Uh, okay." Baffled, Lena waved to Tobias as he jogged back toward his plane.

"Tell Elyse I said hi," Tobias called over his shoulder.

"What about Ian?"

"Tell him he's an asshole."

Lena pursed her lips. Excellent.

Link opened her door for her like a true gentleman, if she could ignore the blazing color of his eyes and the snarl on his lip. He would be a handsome man if he didn't look so feral.

"Sorry," Link muttered as he slid in behind the wheel and shut his door a little too soundly. "It's been a while since I talked to a stranger."

"Link McCall, you said? Of the McCall pack?" The crazy pack that Dalton had told her about.

"Yeah, and clearly you've heard about me already so you don't have to dance around it. It don't bother me. Not anymore."

He spun out of the dirt parking area and onto a long, pothole-riddled road.

"But you're friends with the bears."

"Wild isn't it? Being friends with the enforcers who will put me down someday. The Silvers aren't the bad guys, though." He cast her a wild look. "I am. And when it comes time, I'd rather be put down honorably by one of them than hurt people."

"You don't sound like a bad guy to me," she murmured honestly.

Link dragged his attention from the road to her, then back, but she'd seen it. The grateful look on his face, there and gone.

"I'm a rogue now. The Silvers are the closest I have to a pack, and it makes me feel good to protect Elyse when Ian is sleeping."

"You stay the winters with her?"

Link turned right onto the main road and nodded. "I did for most of the winter last year just in case my family came back for Ian. Elyse was all alone out there defending her mate, and it wasn't right what my pack was doing. And I was there, hunting her, preparing to attack her right along with the rest of my family, but there was this moment. She was standing over her man, firing off round after round, knowing she couldn't win, but she was going to die trying, and she asked me for help. Recognized my hesitation I guess and knew it was me, looked me square in the eyes and begged me. And I couldn't let them hurt a woman who was down for her man like that. It wasn't right."

"You fought your own pack?"

Link nodded once. "Me and Elyse both did, and she took me in after that. She's a loyal sort. Oh, she knows I'm headed straight to hell, but she's determined to take care of me while I'm sane. She's a good person like that. She gave me one of her outbuildings to fix up and stay in. Even kept me fed when hunting and trapping was lean. In return, I kept watch over her place in case my old pack returned. They've scattered to the wind by now, though, so she'll be all right this winter. Tobias had a kill order on one of them this season. Likely, Jenner will have one when he wakes up from hibernation next season. There are a lot of McCalls, and half of us have lost our damned minds already. The bear shifters' handler, Clayton, likes to take turns with them so their animals don't get a taste for the hunt. Bloodlust would be bad on those Silvers." Another long growl sounded from

Link, but stopped abruptly, and he continued as if there had been no interruption at all. "If they go rogue, it would take an army to end one of them. Clayton's right to switch it up every season. You claimed?"

The last question caught her off-guard, so she blinked rapidly and dumbly asked, "What?"

"Tobias sounded like you are important to Jenner. Did he claim you?"

"Y-yes. But he's trying to get me to leave."

Link gripped the wheel and frowned at the road passing beneath his ride. "Why the fuck would he do that? We only pair up once, if we're lucky."

"He's worried I won't be happy here."

Link's face ticked. "Then it's his responsibility to make sure you are."

"The hibernation is what he's hung up on, I think."

"Yeah, well, me and Tobias are working on that." Link clicked his mouth closed with an audible clack, and his eyes went comically blank.

"What did you say?"

"It's Jenner's responsibility to keep you happy."

"Nooo, after that."

"Nothing, and don't ask me again or you're going to get my life ended before I go mad. If Tobias wants you to know what we're working on, he'll tell you his damned self."

Link turned up the radio to an uncomfortable volume and didn't say another word the rest of the trip to Elyse's homestead.

And just below the notes of an old country crooner, Link's feral, wolfish growl rattled on.

Lena would be lying if she said she wasn't intimidated by meeting Elyse. Everyone spoke so highly of her that Lena had drawn up as tight as a guitar string by the time Link pulled in front of a small log cabin. In the yard, a black and white husky with bi-colored eyes barked in a constant fashion.

Link called out, "Quit it, Miki," and the dog trotted over and greeted the werewolf with a friendly lick to the knuckles.

Such a strange sensation washed through Lena as she stood by the open door, scanning the homestead. There was a large fenced cattle pen with one momma cow and her half-grown calf, and beside that was a horse corral with a brown horse who looked to be asleep and a shiny black one who was tossing his head and kicking at nothing as he snorted a pissed-off sound, wary eye on her.

"That's Demon," Link said, jerking his chin toward the horse. "He's crazier than I am."

There was a chicken coop with an outdoor area completely contained in chicken wire, probably to keep out the predator birds from swooping down and making off with them. The soft clucking of hens and the *peep, peep* of chicks filled in a silence that had descended over the homestead when Miki had stopped his barking. And all around the clearing was lush forest the color of vibrant rain-bloated moss.

Her heart was pounding unreasonably fast as her chest filled with some emotion she didn't understand.

"Sounds like they're back in the garden. This way," Link said, striding toward the side of the cabin with a gait too graceful to be human.

Around the corner, Lena skidded to a stop. The garden Link had mentioned was towering with green plants in rows, highlighted with brightly colored vegetables. There was a row of young fruit trees along the back that were producing as well. And in front of a long row of corn stood a couple. The man, Ian she presumed, had his back to them and was holding Elyse off the ground. Her legs were crossed at the ankles, and they were kissing. A flush heated Lena's cheeks at having barged in on such a private moment.

"Come on then," Link said. "They're always doing that."

"Link," Ian said, turning with Elyse in his arms. "I thought I heard—" His eyes went round with surprise when his gaze landed on her. "Hello."

"Link, you dog!" Elyse crowed through a grin.

"No, boss lady, she isn't mine. She's Jenner's."

Elyse landed hard on her feet and swatted her mate. "Oaf, you dropped me!"

"You're Jenner's mate?" Ian asked, his striking blue eyes shocked.

"Yes. Kind of." She pulled at the sleeve of her shirt and tried again. "It's complicated."

Ian strode over to her and pulled the neck of her shirt, no doubt looking for the bite she'd un-bandaged on the way over here. "Holy shit. Where's Jenner?"

"Well, you see, he doesn't know I'm here. He thinks I'm on a plane back to the mainland. He's back at the lodge still."

Ian shook his head and closed his eyes, then blew out a breath. "You've lost me. Let's start from the beginning."

With a grateful smile, she murmured, "Hi, I'm Colleen Rhodes. People call me Lena."

"Ian," he muttered, shaking her hand hard enough to rattle her entire body. "This is my wife, Elyse. So my brother bit you? He just...*bit you*?"

Lena pried her hand from his steely grasp and let off a nervous laugh, then waved shyly to Elyse. "I know what you are and what Link is. I'm just plain and boring human, but I won't tell anyone. About you guys, I mean." She sighed a steadying exhalation. "I love your brother very much, but he has it in his head I don't belong with him."

"Typical Silver," Elyse muttered. Ian cast her a frown, but Elyse said, "What? It's true. Boy scouts, all of you, and so afraid you'll break us." Her delicate eyebrows jacked up. "She doesn't look breakable to me."

"So, what are you doing here then, Lena? Why are you here instead of on that plane?"

"I guess I wanted to talk to Elyse. I want to hear how it really is for her because I have it in my head that I'm in too deep and can't just forget about Jenner, but he's hell-bent on pushing me away. And if it was because he didn't love me back, I would understand—"

"He loves you fine," Ian grumbled. "He fucking bit you. We don't do that if we aren't in it."

"That's what I thought, too, and even if he hadn't claimed me, he said it to me. Right before I left him at the lodge, he told me he loves me."

Link snickered behind her, but when she turned around, he had his arms crossed over his chest and his lips zipped like he wasn't about to let her in on the joke.

"It took Ian forever to admit it," Elyse explained. The honey-haired woman turned and waved her hand for her to follow. "Come on, Lena. You and I have some chatting to do. You boys get dinner on."

"Yes ma'am," Link said with a little salute, but his dove-gray eyes were still dancing and a smile still lingered on his lips. And it wasn't lost on Lena that Link had stopped growling completely around Elyse.

Lena wrung her hands and wiped her damp palms on her jeans.

With a strange look, Elyse asked, "Are you okay?"

"Just nervous."

"To meet me?"

"Well, you're the only other woman in this pack. Crew? Werebear clan?"

"Ha! None of those. The Silver brothers aren't close enough for any of those terms." The smile slipped from her face. "Ian wants it to be different, though. It bothers him they don't talk very much."

"Jenner has nothing but good to say about his brothers. I think it's just the bear part of them."

"Yeah, me too. How did you and Jenner meet?"

And Lena told her. She explained about Adam and her job. About the pictures she was commissioned to take of the brown bears, about Titus, and even how Jenner was her first. She laid it all out there, partly because Elyse was really easy to talk to, and partly because she needed to tell someone all of this just so she didn't have to bear the burden of the confusion alone. And Elyse was an understanding woman. Her green-gold eyes were soft as she walked along beside her down a set of ATV tracks, and she smiled, chuckled, and showed sympathy in all the right places. And it felt so damned good to admit to someone how scared she'd been during Titus's attack, and how hard it had been seeing Jenner at risk to protect her.

Before she could change her mind, Lena said, "Jenner told me about how you got your scar."

Elyse lifted her startled gaze. She was a beautiful woman, and the long, red mark that ran the length of her cheekbone made her look like a warrior. "I would do it all over again if it meant keeping Ian safe," she murmured. "It's hard to look in the mirror sometimes, though."

"Oh, you should be proud of it, Elyse. You're an incredibly brave woman."

She huffed a laugh and bumped Lena's shoulder with her own. "That's what Ian says. He likes the scar. I catch him staring at it sometimes with this look in his eyes that just gets my heart pounding. It's like he doesn't see it as a marring, but an adornment. A trophy maybe. And I'd never admit to him I don't like the way it looks because he would worry. It's not a vanity thing. It's looking at my reflection and always being reminded of that night, you know? I thought we were both goners."

"Is that how it always is for them?" Lena asked softly. "Will I be Jenner's protector?"

"No. Not always. There will be times that are more dangerous for them than others, especially when they carry out kill orders, but Jenner has done just fine fending for himself up until now, right?"

"He says he finds a different den every winter and that he's always concerned a hunter will stumble upon him sleeping. He hibernates around the lodge."

"He does? I thought he was on Kodiak Island or something like Tobias."

"Nope. The guided hunts start in September, and I think he just works until he gets tired and finds a den last minute."

Elyse ran her fingertips absently over her lips as she stared off into the evergreen woods. "Your job requires you to travel, and that is what he is concerned about, too?"

"Yes, but I've emailed my boss, and that can be fixed. Jenner's stuck on the hibernation part. He thinks he can't give me a good life."

"Please. Jenner can afford to provide for a mate, even if you weren't bringing in any income, which you are, so his argument there is completely invalid. He's probably just freaking out like Ian did. It's hard on them to think about going to sleep, not knowing what is happening with us while they hibernate. And it's *hard*, Lena. I'm not going to sugarcoat it. I'm already dreading winter. I'm already dreading the couple of weeks before Ian goes down. He'll start eating more, and we'll be able to tell our time together is coming to an end. I cried for days his first hibernation, and the loneliness is wretched. I would go down into the root cellar where he was sleeping and just lay beside him, because I missed him so much. It's committing yourself to only seeing your mate for half the year. You will grow tough that first winter, and you'll feel that ache of emptiness down to your bones." Lena's heart had grown heavier with every word until Elyse said, "But...summers. Oh, Lena, warm weather is magic. There is nothing like being bonded to a shifter. It would mean complete devotion all your days until the end of your life. There's good and bad, but I can't tell you what to do. You have to decide for yourself whether you are strong enough to be a Silver."

When Miki nudged Lena's palm, she scratched his head. "I'm so tired of running. I didn't even realize it until I came here and spent time in Alaska and connected with an actual place for the first time...ever. I've been living in a hotel, living out of a suitcase, never settling because nothing anchored me. And then I met Jenner, and I realized that maybe home isn't a place at all. That maybe it's Jenner. Even if he's asleep for half the year, I would get the other half. That's the part I can't shake. I can't imagine trying to find someone else. I can't imagine settling, because that's what it would be. I would compare every man to him, and how can anyone stack up? It would be a half-life. Nothing more."

Elyse hugged her shoulders and brought her in close. "Oh, Lena, you have it bad."

"What do I do to convince him I belong with him?"

A slow smile took Elyse's face. "Come on. I have something I want you to see."

FIFTEEN

Two days.

Irritated, Jenner rubbed the palm of his hand back and forth against his forehead, his elbows resting on the dining table as he stared at the picture of Lena on his digital camera. It was the one he'd taken when she was up on the horse, posing and grinning with that beautiful smile of hers.

He'd done right by her, but it didn't make it any less painful now.

Dalton and Chance were on a fishing trip with the bachelor party boys, and Jenner had dipped slowly into madness over the past forty-eight hours with Lennard casting him worried glances every ten minutes.

"I have to show you something," Lennard said, toting his laptop. He opened it on the *Bucks and Backwoods* website. A familiar picture glowed back at him, so Jenner set the camera down and pulled the computer closer. It was a picture of the moose in the pond, and her baby in the background. Beside it was an article about Silver Summit Outfitters.

"She did us proud, boy. And so did you. You really impressed her. I didn't think she wrote articles for them, but they published this one online under their guided trips section. We have the highest rating and are listed at the top. I've had calls all day asking about openings."

Jenner skimmed the article. She'd praised him as the best guide she'd ever worked with, and when he got to the end, to her signature line, he leaned back in the chair, baffled. She had every right to be angry with him, but she'd just boosted his standing in the industry. Why had she gone to the trouble?

"I turned down a couple of immediate tours for you, Jenner," Lennard said quietly.

"Why would you do that? I need to stay busy. Fill me up."

"I think you should take a little time off."

"I take the entire damned winter off, old man."

Lennard leveled him a look with those crinkling blue eyes of his. "This is just your job, Jenner. It's not your whole life." He stood with his gray, bushy brows lifted high on his forehead. "Your brother is on the phone for you."

"Which one?"

"The growly one," Lennard said over his shoulder as he meandered off, laptop tucked under his arm.

Well that narrowed it down.

"Hello," he said into the landline.

"We got an order from Clayton. I need you to come out to the homestead."

"Aw, fuck off, Ian. I'm busy."

"You aren't, and I wouldn't be asking if it wasn't important. Tobias will be there in an hour to pick you up. Pack for a few days." The phone clicked, and the dial tone blasted against Jenner's oversensitive ear. Asshole.

He resisted the urge to slam the phone back in its cradle, but just barely.

Tobias was right on time. Lennard seemed pleased as punch that Jenner was actually taking time off, and everyone was getting on his damned nerves. For the third time, he made sure the camera was in his back pocket so he could take a piece of Lena with him.

The plane ride sucked, naturally, because Tobias smelled like a fucking bear and growled constantly, but on the bright side, Link picked him up so he didn't have to cram himself inside a car with his crazy brother. Just a crazy werewolf instead.

At least he would probably get a good rabbit stew out of the deal. Elyse liked to cook that best, and he hadn't eaten in a couple hours.

"Why are you smiling?" he asked Link suspiciously as he pulled onto the dirt road that led to the homestead.

"Because it's not me you're hunting." Half-truth.

Jenner narrowed his eyes but let it go because he wasn't in the mood to talk to anyone right now, and half-truths reminded him of Mom.

The sun sat low in the sky as Link pulled to a stop in front of the cabin, and Jenner's hackles rose higher when he saw Elyse waiting on the porch for him, her eyes all emotional.

"Are you crying?" he asked, appalled.

"No," she said, her voice squeaky. "I have something in my eye."

"Where's Ian?" Because about now he was ready to bleed whoever Clayton had put out the kill order on.

Elyse pointed down an ATV path that led into the woods. "Down there."

"Are you fucking kidding me?" he muttered, not in the mood for games. "I'm not playing, Elyse. I've had a shit couple of days, and I'm not up for some damned scavenger hunt for my brother."

"Jenner Silver, I will stab you if you don't stop complaining. You want to see your brother? Follow the fucking tracks!"

"Elyse looks pissed," Link murmured. "Just go, okay?"

"Fine," Jenner gritted out, shouldering his backpack. "Later."

He made his way through the trees and, sure enough, there was Ian's scent for him to follow. It was an old trail, though, and the farther away from the house he got, the fainter the scent, which didn't make sense. Up ahead, he could see a light through the trees, and he opened his mouth to yell that Ian better not jump out and try to scare him or he would Change and shred him, but just as he was about to say the first word, another scent hit his nose.

Jenner jerked to a stop and inhaled again. The wind was shifting, so maybe he'd just imagined the body wash Lena had used on the trail. But when the wind righted again, there it was, unmistakable. Heart hammering, Jenner dropped his backpack and began to jog. And when Lena's scent grew stronger, he sprinted forward. In a small clearing surrounding a log cabin, he skidded to a stop.

Lena was standing on the small front porch, surrounded by candle lanterns hanging from pegs. Her hair was down and wavy, two shades darker than the evening sky, and her eyes were full of bottomless emotion.

He reached her in five long strides, hopped over the three stairs, and crushed her to him. "Lena," he murmured between kissing her lips and kissing her cheeks.

She giggled, but it was the thick sort that said she would cry soon if she wasn't already. His Lena.

"What are you doing here?" he asked.

"I have a proposition," she said, hugging his neck and burying her face against his throat.

She felt so damned good against him right now, but when he patted her back, a dust cloud lifted from her sweater. She was filthy from head to toe. "Why are you covered in dirt?"

"Because I was digging."

"Digging what?"

"Your den."

She wasn't making a lick of sense, so he just stared at her, at a loss for words.

"Link and Ian offered to help me dig, but it felt right doing it myself." She tugged his hand and led him off the porch, then around to the side of the house where there was a large opening under the porch. "Ian made sure the cabin was safe over it, though. Look." She squatted down and pointed at the hole.

Jenner looked inside and shook his head, utterly floored by the enormous hole she'd dug. Ian had bolstered the legs of the house with metal, but underneath, the den was as wide as it was deep.

"Lena," he drawled, reality niggling at him.

"Just wait until you hear everything I have to say before you tell me no, Jenner, because this is really important to me, and you said you love me, and if you do, you owe it to me to listen."

Jenner stood slowly, pulling her with him. "Okay."

"I don't like that you pick a different den every year so close to where the boys are running guided hunts. I hate it. It doesn't feel safe."

"Here won't be any safer because Ian will be hibernating too close. The only other time we tried, we went to war as soon as we woke up. Almost killed each other."

"This was Ian's idea."

"It was?"

"Yes! Sort of. Elyse and I kind of planned this, and Ian gave his blessing, even said he liked the idea of you hibernating closer and having a relationship... Anyway, stop interrupting me." She tried to look severe, but failed when she smiled up at him. "Ian said when he woke up last season, it was easy because Elyse had put him in a root cellar and he had plenty to eat as soon as he came to. And I'll do that for you. I'll have food here as soon as you open your eyes, and Bear won't have to feel desperate."

Jenner looked back at the den as the first tendrils of hope filled his chest. "What about your career?"

"I got a promotion."

"You did? Lena, that's great!"

"And then I turned it down."

"What? Why?"

"Because I want to make my home base here, Jenner. I've paid Elyse the first year of rent on this place. It's ours if we want it. And no, I'm not saying you have to quit guiding, but when it gets close to time to hibernate, I propose we come out here."

"To home base."

Lena nodded decidedly. "Yes. To *our* home base."

"But don't you see? This is why I didn't want to do this. You've already turned down a promotion for me."

"Well yes, I turned down that one, but then they gave me another when I explained I wanted to live in Alaska. That's what I was grinning about the other day when I was emailing back and forth with my boss. I'm now *Bucks and*

Backwoods' Photographic Art Director of their Alaska Division. I mean, sure I'll have to beg some plane rides from your brothers during the summer months to cover my responsibilities, and I'll have to use the Wi-Fi in Galena to send in my work, but I won't be giving up anything." She squared up to him and slid her hands up his chest. "And I'll be gaining *everything*. Look, I know you're worried about me when you hibernate, but I won't be alone like Elyse was. I'll have her and Link, and if I get too bored, I can wait until fair weather and travel to the mainland. Pick up a couple of photo jobs. Travel around in the winters if I get the itch. But I'll always, always be back here when you wake up. The hibernation part of this was never a deal-breaker for me, Jenner. Not if it means I get to keep you."

Jenner brushed a wavy strand of her hair from her face and tucked it behind her ear. "This is crazy."

"It's not. It's as normal as we can hope for."

"You really think you can handle all of this?"

"I know I can. For the first time in as long as I can remember, I've never felt surer of anything. I want you. I want to grow our relationship and do this life thing together. And someday, when we're ready, I want to give you cubs."

"But they'll be—"

"Bear shifters. I know and I don't care. We won't be like your parents. We'll make them feel secure and teach them how to be bears the way you and your brothers should've been taught. And I'll love them." Her voice cracked and her face crumpled. "I'll love them so much, and I'll love you even more because I know you'll make a great daddy someday. This is my proposition, Jenner Silver. You already chose me. Now stick with me."

He huffed a shocked sound and shook his head in disbelief that this beautiful woman was claiming him back. She was declaring she wanted *him* to start a life with. She wanted *him* to start a family with. It made no sense, but he was tired of questioning everything. If she could be brave enough to rearrange her entire life for him, then he could be brave enough to make sure she never wanted for anything.

"I'll make you happy," he whispered, resting his forehead against hers.

"I know."

"Marry me then, Lena. If we're going to do this, I want my last name on you."

Tears fell from her eyes, and she clutched his hands. "Well, ask me proper then."

God, he loved her. He *loved* her. She was everything— so much more than he deserved—and she was standing here, offering him something he could've never imagined. All of herself.

Jenner dropped to his knees in the loose dirt she'd dug from his den and lifted his gaze to hers. The sunset was streaking the sky with oranges and pinks behind him, and her cheeks looked rosy in the evening hues. Her shoulders were shaking as she cried, and he thought she couldn't look any lovelier than she did right now, staring down at him, waiting for him to say the words that would bind them for always.

"Lena, I love you more than anything, and I can't imagine my life without you. You're already my mate, but will you do me the honor of being my wife?"

"Yes," she said, nodding. She dashed her damp cheek against her shoulder and said it again, the word that changed his life completely. "Yes, I'll marry you."

Jenner launched upward and picked her up off the ground, holding her tight against his chest. He could feel her heart pounding against him, and he closed his eyes tightly as she laughed a happy tinkling sound.

"I'll buy you a ring. Something pretty. Whatever you want."

Lena laid tiny pecks all over his face before her lips pressed against his. She hugged his neck so tightly as she kissed him, as if she never wanted to let him go, and he understood. He didn't want this moment to ever end. This was the best feeling in the world, declaring a future with her.

"Lena," he murmured, staring at the cabin. "Did you get us a home?"

She was smiling big as she nodded. "Link fixed it up last winter to live in, but he got work in town and bought a place closer to his job. We all pitched in and fixed it just how I wanted it over the last couple of days. Oh, Jenner, I love Elyse, and Ian's so nice, and Link's crazy, but he's awesome, and with the money I paid in rent, Elyse will be able to buy more cattle, and I bought curtains the same blue color of your eyes and a nice mattress because this is our first bed together, and Elyse is going to teach me how to can salmon. And Jenner! Everything just feels so perfect. I get you, and I get a home, and I have two whole months with you before you go to sleep, and we'll make the most out of every moment. Even if I have to tag along on your guided tours and call myself the Silver Summit Outfitters' resident photographer, I will. I *get* to be with you Jenner. I'm the luckiest."

She wasn't, though. His sweet mate didn't see that he was the lucky one.

"Are you happy?" He could see it in her eyes, but damn, he wanted to hear it right now.

"Yes. I never thought I could be so happy. I feel like I finally belong somewhere. You did that, Jenner. I don't have to run anymore."

"You won't ever have to run again. I'll take care of you."

"And I'll take care of you because we are a team."

"Team Silver."

She cupped his cheeks again and laid a lingering kiss on his lips. Easing back, she grinned and whispered, "Team Silver."

SIXTEEN

She couldn't pull her eyes from Jenner. It was his smile, a grin she'd only seen flicker across his face now and again, but here, in the glowing lantern light of their new cabin, it stretched across his lips, transforming his face.

Short, dark scruff graced his jaw, and she ran her fingertips against it. His dark hair had fallen forward over his forehead, making his eyes look even brighter in the fading evening light.

"You haven't shaved since I left," she accused.

"I haven't done much of anything since you left except stare at this picture I took of you."

Her stomach filled with a fluttering sensation that had her melting against him. With a sigh, she rested her cheek against his chest. "Why did you let me leave then? If it hurt so bad, why did you let me go?"

"It's not that I didn't want you, Lena. It's that I wanted better for you."

"Well, that's not how love works, you ridiculous man. You don't set someone free against their will."

Jenner's lips pressed against her hair, lingering as he swayed slowly from side to side. At last, he whispered, "Can I see the cabin?"

Lena nipped his chest, then pulled his hand, leading him up onto the small porch with just enough room for the two rocking chairs that swayed gently in the breeze. She pushed open the door and watched his face as he ducked under the frame and stood to his full height. The smile still lingered at the corners of his lips, but his clear blue eyes pooled with some deep emotion she couldn't fathom. She'd spent the last two days frantically trying to fix it up, but tried to see the cabin from his perspective.

It was split into two primary rooms with smooth wooden floorboards and heavy log walls. There was a single couch in the small living room, right in the shadow of a stone hearth. The butcher-block kitchen counter took up the back wall, speckled with appliances, and on the wall by a two-seater table was a black and white picture of her and Jenner. It was her favorite, and she'd had it printed in Galena today as the finishing touch on this place. She'd thought they were both grinning at the camera when she'd taken it, but while she was cheesing, Jenner had his forehead pressed against her temple, eyes closed like he was taking in the moment with her. They both looked blissfully happy.

Jenner's gaze hesitated on the picture, framed in rough wood, and the emotion in his eyes deepened. God, he was stunning.

"I always wanted a record player, but I haven't stayed in one place long enough," she murmured.

"I'll get you one. We'll find whatever records you want, maybe put it over in that corner," he said, pointing to an empty space near the hearth.

"That's what I was thinking, too. Do you want to see our bedroom?"

"Our bedroom," he repeated softly.

She led the way, but turned at the doorway. "This is my favorite room in the house. As soon as I saw what Link had done, this place just felt like home. Ready?"

Jenner leaned down and sipped her lips softly, then nodded.

Lena pushed open the door and was taken aback all over again. Along one entire wall was a picture window facing the sunset, and on the floor was a large mattress, covered in new, warm, forest green bedding. A small, circular wooden table, grayed with age, sat beside the bed and matched a rustic dresser on the wall opposite the window. Jenner didn't seem to notice anything but the window as he padded toward it.

She held her place near the door just to watch him. She'd imagined it, how he would react, but now that he was really here, this cabin felt complete. He stood against the sunset, his tight black sweater and dark jeans stark against the colors there. Jenner cut a powerful silhouette with his wide, muscular shoulders, tapered waist, and long, commanding legs. When he turned to glance at her over his shoulder, his eyes practically glowed with contentment.

"Come here," he said, holding out his hand, palm up.

The floorboards sounded hollow under her boot steps, and she smiled as her hand slid against his. The cabin had been lifted with metal beams for a reason. "I like the idea that in the winter when I sleep on our bed, you will be hibernating just below me."

Pulling her close to his side, Jenner stared at the colorful streaks across the Alaskan sky. "I'll like sleeping close to you, too."

"Can you imagine it, Jenner? Watching from our bed as the leaves drop in the autumn, and when the first snowfall hits, watching big flurries falling down?" She swallowed hard at the swelling emotion filling her chest. "The second I walked in here, it felt like it was meant to be ours."

Jenner turned her gently in his arms and kissed her, backing her against the smooth wooden wall. Heat flooded her middle as his fingertips brushed up her ribcage to her neck. Angling his face, he slipped his tongue past her lips. A helpless moan filled her chest as she stood on her tiptoes to better reach him. And when the soft rumbling growl that she'd grown to adore vibrated between them, Lena smiled into his kiss. "I love you, I love you, I love you," she whispered.

Leaning forward slightly, Jenner gripped the backs of her knees and lifted her until she was pinned between him and the wall, her legs around him, and his thick erection hard between them. "Woman, I love you, too."

"Never push me away again."

"I can't even if I tried. It's me and you now, Lena. Whatever comes...it's me and you."

His mouth moved smoothly against hers, his tongue brushing hers in a delicious tease. Closing her eyes tightly, Lena gripped his sweater. She could never be close enough to him, and now she understood what Elyse had meant. Winters would be hard and long, but it would make their time together more potent. It would make every kiss and every touch mean more.

Jenner pushed his hips against hers, brushing right where she was most sensitive. His hand gripped the back of her neck as he dropped those nipping kisses to her throat. He sucked hard and ground against her again.

"Jenner," she gasped out on a desperate breath.

He pressed harder against her, then eased off, taking her with him, languidly walking them to the bed. Easily, as if she weighed nothing at all, he lowered them down.

The plush mattress sank under her. Soft bed, hard-as-steel Jenner, encompassing her, blanketing her, making her feel safer than she ever had before. Lena arched back against the comforter as he lifted off her just enough to remove his shirt. His hair came out mussed and sexy, and she ran her hands through it just to touch him. His arms flexed as he lowered himself to her, and with his teeth, he pulled the bottom of her sweater up her stomach, brushing her skin lightly as he rucked it up. The second his lips brushed her ribs, she shivered.

A deep chuckle reverberated from him. "You like that, don't you?"

Breath hitching, she nodded and pushed his head gently lower. The smile he flashed her was nothing shy of wicked before he pulled her jeans down her hips and let them slip from his fingertips onto the floor. Lena hadn't ever done this with anyone else, but she was safe with Jenner. Safe to try what she wanted, safe to ask for what she wanted. He moved farther down and kissed the inside of her knee, running his hand up her outer thigh. Her breath was shaking now, but the nervous flutters in her stomach only added to her anticipation. Slowly, he worked his way up the inside of her leg with those sexy lips of his until he clamped his teeth gently onto her inner thigh. She gasped and rolled her hips toward him. Hands sliding under her hips, he pulled her closer to him and ran his tongue the length of her seam, then lingered on her clit, sucking gently, encouraging her to spread her knees wider for him.

He laved his tongue against her again, teasing. How could anything feel so good? Lena rocked against him, fingers gripping his hair as she bowed her neck back and whispered his name. When his soft humming growl vibrated from his throat against her clit, she nearly lost it completely. Jenner slid his tongue inside of her, and she was gone. Couldn't think. Couldn't do anything other than heed the pace he set and move against him as the pressure in her middle built. Over and over he pushed into her until she tipped over the edge completely. Lena cried out as an orgasm crashed through her.

"Need to feel you come," he gritted out.

And before her aftershocks had even subsided, he was undressed. Up on locked arms, staring into her eyes with such hunger, Jenner slid his swollen cock deep into her. Chest heaving, he closed his eyes and froze as she pulsed softly around him. Only when her orgasm was completely finished did he move, slowly at first, and the pressure in her middle began to build again.

The second she clamped her teeth gently over his pec, Jenner turned them over and sat up. Straddled around him, connected so deeply, Lena gripped the back of his hair and rolled her hips, setting their pace now. He'd given her control. This big, dominant, growly, strong man had pushed Bears instincts to the side so that she could have her way here in their den.

Jenner hugged her tightly as his body contracted and relaxed, contracted and relaxed. He was strung impossibly tight, and he gritted out her name as he swelled within her. So close now. When Lena sucked gently on his earlobe, the growl in his chest turned feral. He buried his face against her neck, but she wanted him to see how he owned her, body and soul.

"Look at me," she whispered, pulling the back of his hair until those intense, darkening eyes of his were steady on her. She bit his bottom lip as punishment when he closed his eyes, and when he opened them again, they were dark as pitch. "My bear."

She slid over him again, and his body contracted and held. He gritted out a snarl and froze inside of her. Throbbing jets of seed shot into her, over and over as her own release pounded through her. Jenner spun her so fast her stomach dipped. He pressed her against the bed, then slammed into her with a helpless groan. God she loved him like this. Dominant. Primal. Barely in control as he emptied himself completely into her. And when his pace slowed and smoothed out, when he buried his face against her neck and his breathing had steadied, she dragged her fingernails lightly up and down his back, her face stretching with a happy smile.

"I thought I lost you," he murmured against her throat.

"Never."

Jenner eased out of her and lay behind her, big spoon to her little spoon. Propped up on one elbow behind her shoulder, Jenner leaned forward and kissed her cheek.

"Are you watching the sunset with me?" she asked, as quiet as a breath. The final colored streaks were adorning the horizon in deep, fiery colors.

"No. I've seen a hundred sunsets. I don't want to take my eyes off you."

Happiness unfurled in her belly as she snuggled closer against him. She lifted his hand from her hip to her lips and let her kiss linger on his knuckles. "Jenner?"

"Yeah?"

"I'm glad Bear chose me."

With a single, soft laugh, Jenner brushed his scruff against her cheek once, then whispered, "How could he not? Loyal, protective, beautiful, strong woman. You're everything I could've wanted in a mate."

"Can I tell you something?"

"Anything," he rumbled.

As the last streaks faded from the evening sky, she sighed and pulled his hand against her cheek. "I miss you already."

Jenner was quiet for so long she turned in his arms to face him. He rested his cheek on his arm and brushed a strand of hair from her face. "For the first time since my first hibernation, I hate that part of myself." His eyes tightened as he brushed his gaze over her hair, then back to her eyes. "I don't want to do it."

Lena gave him a reassuring smile and ran her hand down his side. His tan skin was webbed with the silver scars Tobias had given him all those years ago. Her mate—so strong, but allowing her to see a side of him he shared with no one else.

"It makes no difference if you have to go to sleep or not," she whispered, holding his gaze so he could see the honesty of her words. "I'll be here when you wake up. Always."

Jenner hugged her tightly against him, his heart beat steady and strong against her cheek. And as the shadows lengthened across the room—their room—he murmured the words that had become medicine for her soul. Words that she would never tire of hearing because they'd gone through so much to get right here. "I love you, Lena."

And because of his devotion, their future together now stretched on and on. He had come in and pushed her barricaded heart open. The changes and growth she'd gone through had been painful and scary, but with Jenner, she'd finally felt like she could close her eyes and jump off the edge, knowing he would catch her. Today was the first day of the rest of their lives. And as she pressed her lips against his warm skin, his earlier words brushed her mind.

Whatever comes...it's me and you.

For the first time in her life, she didn't feel alone. She wasn't a ship lost at sea.

From now until forever, Jenner would be her anchor, as she would be his.

EPILOGUE

Lena cocked her head and readjusted the large picture over the bed until it was straight. There was no headboard, so she'd decided to make a photo montage of differently sized and shaped pictures across the back wall instead. They were all black and white prints of her and Jenner's wedding day.

Her gaze drifted to the picture window. Outside, the ground was covered in white, and the branches of the towering evergreens were covered in snow. Large flakes fell from the gray sky in a constant downpour. It was beautiful, but more than that, it was haunting. Sadness bloomed in her chest as she ripped her attention away from the wintery landscape. A piece of her would always hate snow now.

It had been one month since Jenner had gone to sleep. One month that felt like a year as each day dragged. Twice already, she'd given in and curled up under the house with him in her warmest winter clothes just to be close to him—her silver-furred bear.

Elyse had warned her over and over, but Lena had no way to mentally prepare for how long hibernation actually lasted. Six months didn't sound so bad before the snow. One, two, three, four, five, six, and it would be done. She would be reunited with Jenner. But when each day dragged on for eternity, it was a different story.

The pictures scattered across the bed around her feet were an escape. This project was a way to remember how good things had been, and how good they would be again.

Soft notes sounded from the record player in the living room, and Lena reached forward, brushed her fingertip lightly over the enormous print above the mattress.

Her and Jenner's wedding had been at the lodge in late September, and the first snow had decided to show up that day. Mom and Lena's sisters had traveled all the way to Alaska for it and fretted over the weather for two days before the wedding, but not her. The falling snow made the most beautiful photographs.

This picture over the bed was the only one taken of her and Bear. Jenner had allowed her one, after all the wedding guests had gone inside except for Elyse. Lena had found a quiet place in the woods and set up the shot on a tripod, then

Elyse had taken the picture with an old film camera. In the oversize print, she wore her fitted wedding dress, covered in crystals with a long flowing train, just like she'd always imagined when she was a little girl. The light train whipped in the wind, and though Lena faced the camera, her head was turned, as if she was waiting. Because she was. Behind her, barely visible through the falling snow, Bear was walking toward her.

Jenner had built her a darkroom on the back of the house, and she'd developed every one of these prints herself. In one, Link and the Silver brothers laughed, looking dapper in their dark suits on the deck of the lodge overlooking the snowy river. In another, Mom was wiping a snowflake off Lena's cheek. One was of Jenner's face when she'd first come out of the lodge in her dress. Eyes raw and open, Jenner looked at her as if he'd never seen anything more beautiful. Elyse had clicked away on Lena's camera, capturing incredible pictures of their special day. Lena and Jenner slow dancing in the snow. Link watching the Dawsons warily with his wolf-bright eyes. Tobias and Ian talking, hands in their pockets. She and Jenner's first kiss as the snow fell around them. Lennard, Dalton, and Chance grinning right at the camera, all with bunny ears behind their heads.

One by one, each photo she'd developed in the chemicals in her dark room were exposed as treasures.

A bark rang out, and Lena tilted her ear toward the front of the house. Link sometimes ran these woods as a wolf, just to make sure all was well, but he rarely even yipped. Must be Miki, which meant Elyse was on her way over. With a grin, Lena set down a picture of Mom crying and smiling as she hugged Jenner's shoulders. In a rush, Lena bolted for the living room and turned down the record player, then threw the door open.

Only Elyse looked panicked and was sprinting toward her in a heavy jacket and snow boots.

"What's wrong?" Lena called out, reaching for the rifle over the door. If something was after Elyse, she would be ready to protect her friend.

Miki was bounding in the snow near Elyse's feet, barking over and over, clearly agitated by whatever had Elyse running so fast.

"Turn on the radio," Elyse cried.

"It's on! What's happened?"

Elyse took the porch stairs two at a time and just about fell in through the front door. Miki came in, too, but at least he quit his barking. Now he was licking at Elyse's fingers, trying to console her.

Winded, Elyse locked her hands on her knees and gasped out, "Tobias."

Panic flared in Lena's chest. "What about him? Is he hurt? Elyse! Talk to me!"

She lifted her gold-green eyes to Lena and said, "He radioed the house."

"What?" Lena looked outside at the falling snow. It was mid-November, way past when the boys went down for hibernation. "Why is he still awake?"

Elyse shook her head and stood up straight, taking long, deep breaths. "I don't know. I asked him, but he said he wouldn't say another word until I was with you. He said he was going to radio over here."

Baffled, Lena checked the radio, but she already knew it was on. That's how she and Elyse talked when the weather was too bad to travel the mile to each other's cabins.

"Lena," the radio chirped out. It was really Tobias. "You there?"

She ripped the speaker off the box and pushed the button. "Yeah, I'm here. So is Elyse."

"Let me hear her."

"I'm here," Elyse said into the speaker, then shrugged her own bafflement at Lena. "How are you still awake? Did someone hurt you?"

"No, I never went to sleep. Listen, I wanted to try this on myself before I put Ian and Jenner at risk."

"What are you talking about, Tobias?" Elyse asked, voice frantic.

"You two go start putting food in their dens. I'm coming to you. I'll be there in three days. I'm going to wake my brothers up."

"Wake them up?" Elyse whispered, her eyes gone round. "Tobias, you can't. They're hibernating."

"I owe them, Elyse. I *owe* them. I knew I had to fix this when you were attacked by the McCalls and we couldn't do a damned thing about it. You wouldn't have that scar on your face if we were awake to protect you. And Jenner—" Static blasted across the line. "Lena, I owed it to him to try. I hurt him."

Lena shook her head at Elyse's confused look and grabbed the speaker. "Tobias, we don't understand. And Jenner isn't mad for what happened when you were kids. You didn't mean to hurt him. Just...tell us what's happening."

Elyse was crying, but Lena didn't understand why. She just hugged her friend tightly and waited for Tobias to tell them what the hell was going on.

245

"You'll never have to worry about winter again," he said. "You'll never have to wait for your men to wake up."

Elyse was sobbing against her now with her hands clasped over her mouth, body shaking. Tears slid down Lena's cheeks in rivers as a thin thread of hope wound around her heart.

"Say it, Tobias," Lena demanded thickly. "Say it now before we fall apart."

Seconds ticked by, and at last the radio static disappeared. Tobias's voice wavered with emotion as he murmured, "I've found a cure."

The End

Want More of These Characters?

Up Next in This Series

Mate Fur Hire
(Bears Fur Hire, Book 3)

Sneak Peek

Chapter One

Tobias Silver threw open the door of the Galena Post Office and wiped his muddy boots on the mat inside. July in Alaska meant warm weather and sunshine, but it also meant the main drag in town was often a swamp thanks to the summer rains.

The scent of werewolf hit his nose immediately, and he threw a suspicious glance over at a bench along the wall. Half-shadowed by a full coat rack, Lincoln McCall sat there, one leg stretched out as though he'd been waiting a while. His crazy wolf eyes blazed as his gaze followed Tobias to the front desk.

"What the fuck do you want?" Tobias asked in a barely audible voice that the humans waiting in line wouldn't hear but Link would pick up just fine.

"Hello to you, too," Link growled out, striding toward Tobias, his boots echoing across the wooden floor. "Took you long enough to come pick up this package."

Tobias tossed him a withering look as the man stood beside him with his arms crossed. "I have shit to do, dog. Back-to-back deliveries mean I can't just drop everything to make a trip out here for a single package."

"I've been waiting for two days."

"What? Why? You should've just called me if you wanted something."

"On the radio?" Link's dark eyebrows shot up, and his gray eyes blazed brighter. "That's what you must mean because you never pick up your damned phone. I know because I called it a dozen times, and what I have to say shouldn't be talked about over the radio waves."

Mickey Gunderson, the postmaster, waved him forward as a little old lady shuffled off with a package in her hands. "Tobias Silver, this package is a fragile one."

When he disappeared into the back room, Tobias leaned heavily on the countertop angled away from Link, who was standing too damned close.

"You'll want to hear what I have to say," Link murmured. "It could possibly save your family a lot of grief."

"What do you care about my family?"

"Are you kidding me right now? I'd do anything for Elyse. Anything for Ian. Hell, if Jenner asked me for a favor, I'd do it." A long growl rattled Link's throat, and he shook his head hard to stifle the sound. Crazy wolf.

Tobias narrowed his eyes at him. Link had spoken each word with such conviction, he had to be telling the truth. Because of his heightened shifter senses, Tobias could tell a lie. "Why, Link? I honestly want to know why you care about them so much. You remember what happened to your brother, don't you?"

Link's face went blank, and red crept up the sides of his neck. "Yeah, I know what happened to Cole, and he wanted it, you snarky asshole. You think he wanted to be hurting people? Ian did him a fucking favor, just like he'll do for me someday. And I'll die with honor because Ian is my friend." Link turned to leave but circled back and lowered his voice. "You don't even know how lucky you are, Silver." Link's glowing gaze locked on his for a moment more before he strode outside, slamming the door after him.

Huh. Tobias twirled a pen between his fingers and frowned. Link had abandoned his pack the day they went after Elyse. The day they scarred up her face and tried to kill Ian when he was mid-hibernation. Link had fought his own family to protect them. Tobias had never understood his reasons, but he did know one thing. Werewolves didn't do well rogue. They needed packs, and from the way Link talked about Ian and Elyse, it dawned on Tobias. Link wasn't rogue. He'd just chosen a different pack, albeit a broken one. With a bear shifter and a human, this make-shift pack was one that shouldn't work by any means, but apparently they were all Link had now, and he was going to stick with them until he went mad, just like every other McCall had done since the beginning of their lineage.

Regret slashed through Tobias's chest. He didn't hate Link. In fact, he actually liked the idiot, but someday, Ian was going to be called on to kill his friend, and the unfairness of that was a mighty blow. Tobias might not get along with his brothers much, but that didn't mean he wanted them hurt. And killing Link was going to hurt Ian.

Tobias muttered a curse and scrubbed a hand down his face. This right here was why he had stalled coming to Galena. Ian and Elyse, and even Link, lived too close. They brought up all these emotions he didn't know what to do with, pain he didn't understand, and now his inner bear was writhing in his middle, snarling to be released.

You don't even know how lucky you are.

Link was so wrong.

"Here it is," Mickey said, grunting under the heavy weight of an oversize box that had masking tape wrapped around it several dozen times. "I think Ian was meant to take it, but he's swamped with deliveries right now, and he and Elyse are talking about driving their cattle back early, and they are fighting a war with the mice near their garden, and one of their goats just had twins but she won't feed one of them—"

"Mickey!" Damn, he knew this was a small town, but did everyone know everything about everyone?

"Oh, right. They're your family. You already know all this."

Actually he didn't, and now he felt even shittier, *thank you, Galena.*

Mickey hoisted the box onto the counter with a great groan, then said, "You ever delivered to Perl Island before?"

And there it was. The final rub of this shit-tastic trip. Perl Island, one of the most dangerous places on earth. The Alaskan weather liked to dump all of her violence right over the island. If he was lucky enough to land safely, then he would have to deal with the natives. That strip of land was known in his world as the Island of Misfit Shifters.

"Yes, I have." Once, and it didn't go well.

"Well, good luck to you."

Tobias grunted his thanks and pulled the package off the counter. It was light as a feather to him, but he'd learned long ago that people don't like seeing his shifter strength. It made humans uncomfortable. So he acted like it was heavy, gave Mickey Gunderson a polite smile, and made his way out the door.

Link was waiting outside, leaned up against the log wall of the post office. "I'm going with you."

"What? No." Tobias sauntered right past him and down the porch stairs.

"The lady you're delivering that to? She's a witch."

Tobias barely resisted the urge to growl at him as he turned right onto the main road that led out of town toward the landing strip where his bush plane was waiting. He walked faster, but Link lengthened his stride and kept up.

"Why do you think Perl Island works so well for the misfits? Huh? Think about it. Clayton hasn't given you a kill order on any of them, and they're all crazy."

"Not McCall level crazy."

"Maybe not, but maybe so."

Tobias cast him a quick glance. He hadn't thought about it before, but Link was right. Clayton Reed, his handler, had never sent him out there to even punish a shifter for stepping out of line. And to his knowledge, Ian and Jenner hadn't been given orders on Perl Island either. "Tell me what you're talking about quick before I lose my patience."

"There's a lady on the island who has them all in line. They don't need outside intervention because she's managing every one of those crazy shifters. All of them, Tobias." He gave him a significant look. "How is one woman doing all that?"

"Hell if I know."

"She's suppressing their animals."

"Oh, come on, Link. That's rumor. That shit has been flying around for years. She isn't a witch, and she's not suppressing animals. The misfits are just staying in line so people stay off their land and leave them alone."

"I thought so, too, but then something changed."

"What changed?"

"I found her." Link's voice was growing more and more excited. "I tracked her down—her name and how I could reach her—and I made a call. Tobias, I talked to her, and you know what she told me when I asked her if she could help shifters with out-of-control animals?"

Fine, out of curiosity, he would play along. "What did she say?"

"She said she won't talk to anyone but you, but that I wasn't wrong."

"Me? I don't know anyone on Perl Island. What does she want with me?"

"To hire you. She said she needs you for an important job."

"Fuck, Link! You're getting sucked into this elaborate hoax, man!"

Link jerked Tobias's arm and squared up to him, eyes blazing. "If you were me and you had a shelf life because you could feel your animal taking over. If you knew you were going to die at the claws of one of your friends. If you knew you would want to hurt people because you're going mad, wouldn't you try? I need this, Tobias. I need to make sure I tried everything before I just give up and give in. And I know that sounds selfish, but I didn't just contact the witch for me. You weren't there when Elyse was bleeding and standing over Ian's body. Your brother's body! I could see it in her eyes. She knew she was going to die, and still, she popped round after round into my pack, protecting him. That should've never happened. You Silvers shouldn't be hibernating. You want to know why I really care about your family? Elyse is good, Tobias. I mean really good to her bones, and I'm lucky enough to get to be around someone like that. And Ian is a match for her. I'll stay saner longer just for knowing them. I was part of the pack that hunted her. Hunted. Her. And then she took me in, gave me a place to live on her property, fed me when food got low at the end of winter, and she told me I am good. No one has ever said that to me! I'm not just asking you to go meet with this woman because I want to live. I'm asking so we can rule out any chance of Ian staying awake this winter so Elyse doesn't have to be alone. Because when I die, and oh, I can feel the madness coming—when I go, who will watch her while Ian sleeps?"

Tobias shook his head over and over in denial of what Link was saying because it did him no good for Tobias to build up hope. There wasn't a cure. It didn't exist, but Link was staring at him with such desperation and dammit, Tobias owed him since he'd been a part of saving Elyse and Ian last winter. Link had talked about how good Elyse was, but Link had kept her safe, patrolling her property all winter to make sure the remaining McCalls didn't come back for her and her mate's hibernating body. Elyse was right. Link *was* good, or as good as a half-crazed werewolf could be.

"Fuck," he muttered. "What's this lady's name?"

"Vera Masterson."

At the sound of her name, a strange, warm feeling unfurled in Tobias's chest and made it hard to draw a breath. "Doesn't sound like a witch name to me."

"So you'll do it?"

Tobias let off a long, irritated sigh. "On two conditions."

"Name them."

"I go alone. Whatever trap I'm walking into, I don't want you involved. I'll call you when it's done."

"And the second condition?"

Tobias leveled him with a hard look. "You don't tell anyone about this, and you don't get your hopes up."

"Why not?"

Tobias turned and strode toward the edge of town, adjusting the package in his grasp as he went. Over his shoulder he called, "Because there is no cure."

Mate Fur Hire

(Bears Fur Hire, Book 3)

About the Author

T.S. Joyce is devoted to bringing hot shifter romances to readers. Hungry alpha males are her calling card, and the wilder the men, the more she'll make them pour their hearts out. She werebear swears there'll be no swooning heroines in her books. It takes tough-as-nails women to handle her shifters.

Experienced at handling an alpha male of her own, she lives in a tiny town, outside of a tiny city, and devotes her life to writing big stories. Foodie, wolf whisperer, ninja, thief of tiny bottles of awesome smelling hotel shampoo, nap connoisseur, movie fanatic, and zombie slayer, and most of this bio is true.

Bear Shifters? Check
Smoldering Alpha Hotness? Double Check
Sexy Scenes? Fasten up your girdles, ladies and gents, it's gonna to be a wild ride.

For more information on T. S. Joyce's work,
visit her website at
www.tsjoycewrites.wordpress.com

Made in the USA
Charleston, SC
15 October 2016